The Passionate Past of Gloria Gaye

Bernard Kops

Secker & Warburg · London

First published in England 1971 by
Martin Secker & Warburg Limited
14 Carlisle Street, London W1V 6NN

Printed in Great Britain by Northumberland Press Limited
Gateshead

For Erica

I

'Where there's death there's hope,' Gloria reassured herself and giggled, but she did not throw herself under the bus; instead she crossed the road just as carefully as everyone else.

Sometimes one had to carry on, and there probably were many good reasons for continuing this existence, though as she approached her destination she could not think of even one; so she giggled again.

The National Gallery towered over her, but that was all to the good because it shielded her from the horrible north-east wind that was blowing all the way from the Arctic Circle, down Monmouth Street, and right into Trafalgar Square.

Soon she would go home. After this feast of art she would once again return to her home sweet honeycomb, deep in the kind forest of Soho. Meanwhile, she entered into the oasis of the National Gallery, and avoided looking right or left as she walked straight to the far room where her beloved picture was hanging.

Her beloved Flora. It had been painted by Mr Rembrandt when he was acted by Mr Charles Laughton, in those days when Hollywood made pictures.

'Flora.' Gloria might have been looking into a mirror, so she sat down near to it and just looked into it, and she just knew that she could have hit it off very well with Mr Rembrandt; had she lived in that Amsterdam of long ago.

The face was sad yet courageous; it had dignity and tranquillity.

There were certain faces that still existed in this city. Faces that made you feel safe. Faces that were stepping-stones in the great black river of engulfing darkness. Faces where you found spiritual succour and release from the past and the future.

Gloria was a little angry with herself for coming here. Five minutes' walk from that mental home in Surrey there had been a station. Those little electric trains stopped there every fifteen minutes, and she had been shot from there right into the heart of Charing Cross. She had tried to go direct to the ultimate security of her street door, but that had proved impossible. But now she was pleased that she had broken her journey, for Flora was a sight for sore eyes; and certainly a sight for a sore mind.

No, she did not mind calling that place a mental home. The whole world was full of euphemisms these days; the whole world was calling the whole world by names that were really not its own. But she could face it and had been much more relieved since she'd started calling a spade a spade.

And she did not mind thinking back over her stay at that place, and of the events that led her into that place, as she sat in the centre of the greater mental home called Greater London.

'So, it was the book that led to the breakdown?' the voice of Mr Moss boomed through the empty Rembrandt room. She could practically see him sitting beside her, as he so often did on the grass of Surrey, up until that same morning before she left those gates of the

8

mental home forever. Gloria looked at her watch and found it incredible to accept that only two hours before she had been within those gates, and still officially within the throes of breakdown.

'So, it was the book that led to the breakdown?' the invisible voice repeated. When she first met Mr Moss she thought that he was a doctor, his eyes had pierced right inside her; and his voice. And all those days that she had been in that place, she had attached herself only to him. Some people were like that, they could not help being very special.

'No, it wasn't the book, Mr Moss, it was the death of the book,' she said it then and she said it now.

'I'm sorry, I didn't read it.'

His voice always seemed to pin her down, and now she realized how much she would miss him. He was a pure, beautiful man, and horrible thoughts never crossed his mind. She was sure of that. He was not cursed with the horrible creeping cancerous disease that crept over most men's minds; that terrifying incessant lust.

'Sex! Sex! Sex!' That's all they thought or cared about. But Mr Moss had proved himself different.

She came back to the surface of Flora for a moment, and because she didn't want to weep she laughed again. Tragedy always affected her like that; and besides, it was easier that way. If you cried people became mad, but if you laughed people merely thought you were mad.

'So what went wrong with the book? Why didn't it have a fantastic reception?'

She stood up to reply and looked down to where Mr Moss might have been, and where he probably was, on that grass, still within the gates of that madhouse in

Surrey. 'I expect all those intellectual hermaphrodites, who review anything but their lives every Sunday, simply could not take the romantic reality of me. You know the trend, you know what is wanted nowadays. Filth! Smut! And slime! I wasn't kinky enough for them, Mr Moss. I wasn't perverted! I wasn't pornographic.' She looked around the room. Some straggling Scandinavians were staring through their glasses, but she was glad that she had not been followed from the station; or if she had, she was certainly delighted that she had managed to give him the slip.

He would have to get up very early in the morning to keep up with her, whoever he was.

'Yes, romance followed God into the grave. And the book went down the drain as soon as it was published.'

'So you weren't happy with your publishers?'

'Publishers!' Her ridicule exploded and shattered the silence. 'What do they know? It was far too sad and beautiful for most of them. Consequently, in order that my autobiography was not consigned to absolute oblivion, I was compelled to allow a dear, drunken friend to publish it.'

'I didn't know it was an autobiography,' she emulated his voice inside her mind, because she wasn't absolutely sure that she had actually had this conversation with him.

'The odd thing was that nobody took it as my true life story. Everybody thought it was a novel. And that silly sod of a publisher didn't make it any easier. Mind you, he is the very best third-rate publisher there is. It's true he works in one room in Fitzroy Square and sleeps on the floor with his secretary. Nevertheless, I did not have to pay him to publish the book, though now I wish it had never come out.'

10

'Why didn't they believe it was an autobiography? Didn't it say so?'

'Yes, but you couldn't really blame them. Who could believe the reality of my life? You must admit it is quite fantastic. Besides, nobody believes anything nowadays. Have you read my book, Mr Moss?'

He shook his head and she slowly handed him a copy. 'I really wish that you wouldn't. I want you to judge me for what I am, not for what I was.'

She still felt completely split about the book. Ever since it had been published she had felt delighted and nauseated; thrilled yet exposed.

But then again, all her life she had had to walk the slender tightrope strung between the many extremes of her emotions. She was thankful that so far she had been quite clever in keeping her balance. Anyway the problem was solved, for Mr Moss immediately put the book into a pocket that seemed to swallow it all up.

'If you know anyone who wants to buy six hundred beautifully bound copies of my life story...' She had bought them very cheaply from her publisher friend and no wonder she had gone almost insane when they had been delivered to her. Belton Psychiatric Hospital had certainly been a sanctuary from the world. Whoever could have thought that one could find refuge in Surrey? And then she recalled that once she had lived amongst the grassy slopes of that purified county. But in those days she had been dead.

'I must remind you, Mr Moss, that I was a voluntary patient and I am not ashamed of this address, provided it has helped me in some way.'

He nodded like a fairground plaything, and Gloria realized that she knew practically nothing about him. 'Were you committed, Mr Moss?'

11

'No, I was commuted.' He had thick grey hair. It was very distinguished-looking and it had a very strong texture. She longed to touch him, to stroke his hair.

The Scandinavians were also looking at Flora now. They stood before it in that strangely idiosyncratic stupid manner of connoisseurs. But she didn't really want them to slip over and fall upon their faces; and she was sure that they were not wearing disguise. One of them was definitely a man, and the other was definitely a woman. And they definitely came from Stockholm or Oslo, or Copenhagen, and neither of them had followed her into this place, neither singly nor together. And they would not follow her out.

Nevertheless she was glad that her conversation with Mr Moss was taking place inside herself, so she continued quite safely.

'Anyway, it was nice being with you for those few weeks, Mr Moss.'

He laughed. It was unusual for him. 'Miss Gaye, you are always making the same mistake, and one doesn't know if it is unintentional or deliberate. You've been here at least six months.'

'Mr Moss, I like you despite your incredible imagination.'

'You came in here before me. Don't you remember? I practically followed you into this place.'

'Anyway, two weeks away from my home is long enough. And so I must be going. Please visit me, Mr Moss, if you're passing.'

'I shall come and call on you.'

She wrote down her address and handed it to him. But because he was not there she would put it into her pocket. It was always good to carry your address in your pocket, it made you feel safe because it reminded you of where you belonged in the universe.

'Thank you, I shall come sooner than you think.' He scanned the address and put it in the pocket.

'I'll expect you,' she could not resist leaning over and kissing him lightly on the cheek. He smelled so . beautifully, so much of himself. He smelled the colour of peace. Of damp wood. She wished that she had kissed him before leaving that place, because all she could do now was kiss the empty air. 'Guess how old I am?'

His trepidation was remarkably sincere, and he moved his hand as if bartering. 'Forty ... five?' He seemed hurt in case he had raised the amount too high.

She laughed gratefully and decided to be honest. 'Actually I'm a little older than that. I am in that no man's land between forty-five and sixty-five and I think that I shall stay there.'

'Wherever you are, whoever you are, and however old you are, I shall call on you, I promise.'

It was time to leave, because a bell was ringing either in Surrey or in Trafalgar Square, and a mist was pouring down into the National Gallery. And the tourists were noiselessly shuffling out.

She went close to her beloved Flora and it was just like gazing at her own most beautiful reflection.

It was necessary to love oneself, eventually; at least some of the time. She would go now. She would walk right through the walls of the art gallery, and she would brave Charing Cross Road. She would walk above all the longing, frozen dead who gazed up from beneath those paving stones; she would go north towards Covent Garden, to the beautiful smell of rotting oranges and cauliflowers. She would walk upon her usual tightrope above the upward funnelling faces, through the thick conserve of traffic and a delicatessen of flesh. She would pass the luncheon-voucher faces staring out from their Wimpy glass. But above all, she would exorcise her endless and incredible headache as soon as she reached her street door, where she would be greeted by her lodgers and receive the few weeks' back rent that was owing her.

'Goodbye, Mr Moss. Goodbye.'

Gloria turned and waved, but the attendants seemed to understand and did not smile stupidly.

'I shall follow you, Miss Gaye. I'll come very soon. Sooner than you think.'

His voice got fainter and fainter now and she knew that she was alone. No one was waiting outside the gallery, lurking behind the columns, and no one was loitering in the street pretending to read a newspaper. There were just the usual dead, slowly flowing by. It was quite safe to descend into the street. So she did, and decided to bend with the decaying wind and go with them for a while.

She reached Cambridge Circus, but instead of going straight towards her home, she decided to turn left. It was a sudden impulse from the throbbing heart of Soho that made her change her mind. And in the noon moon or the light night it made no difference. The sky was always the same. She was no longer afraid of her dead relatives, you couldn't hide from them anyway; those alive and those in the grave who were now floating horizontal in the sky. So she watched them pass from east to west and waved back at them.

And she could manage perfectly well without her daughter. Angela was a stranger and they had nothing in common. She would avoid her daughter like the plague.

Gloria loved Soho. Here the natives were once

friendly, and she hoped that nothing had changed in a few weeks.

'Six months indeed. He must have been out of his mind,' and Gloria laughed, because she realized that Mr Moss was out of his mind. 'It's just as well you were around the twist or I would not have met you, and you would not be coming to see me.'

But now it was time to take some time off from rehearsing for death or life; or whatever oblivion was known by nowadays. And she walked to where the York Minster, her favourite pub, used to be.

'You never know, civilizations disappear in a few weeks these days.'

'What did you say, lady?' the vendor asked.

'A bag of chestnuts please.'

Gloria took them and gave him the money. She loved the smell of hot chestnuts and she stood for a moment in Old Compton Street, just sniffing at the bag that she held to her nose. And then she threw the bag away. They would probably have been all wormy, and she couldn't afford to take any more chances. So she hurried now towards the public house that was just around the corner. It was stretching out its arms and hands to her, right round the corner; it was calling her home. It was waiting to pour the hot necessary milk of noon down into her thirsty dehydrated throat.

She hurried to turn that corner, though she looked back over her shoulder.

Today indeed was her lucky day, for no one, absolutely no one had followed her. And all she had to do, now that she was back again in the world, was to untie the tight band clamped around her forehead and practically bursting her head.

2

She stopped before entering, to calm herself, and to allow that band to expand; that invisible band held tightly by the cold hand of that absentee landlord Mr God.

A cat snaked and purred around her legs so she stopped to stroke it. Obviously it had not heard the bad news, and she didn't feel like purveying disillusion.

'Sweet little pussy, my precious. You think the whole universe is for you. And so it is, and you're simply waiting to take over the world.' They certainly could not have made a worse job.

Then she entered the warm crowded interior, but she didn't recognize anyone, except the assistant who smiled. 'Hello, Miss Gaye, haven't seen you for so long. Been on holiday?'

'Yes...' she had forgotten the name that went with the face. But some faces were like that; they had no names.

'Madeira was rather charming, but Tenerife was a rubbish dump.' Gloria wiped a tear from her eye. 'Sooner or later I really must do something about this generous aqueduct of mine.'

The face smiled vacantly. 'Anyway Miss Gaye, it's good to see you again.'

'And how's your lady wife?'

'But Miss Gaye, you know I'm not married.'

The man was obviously mad. How convenient it was to lose a wife all of a sudden. She looked up at the clock and smiled back at him. 'Something rather nice, like ... no, I'll have a pink gin.'

No sooner said than done. And it tasted excitingly bitter. So she savoured it.

'Horace my love, my sweet darling, how divine to see you.'

The man, who did not wear his years exceptionally well, turned slowly towards her.

'Why hello, Gloria, I'm so happy to see you.' He kissed her but she did not show her shudder.

'What are you drinking?' He ordered more drinks for both of them, using his own intimate sort of sign language.

'Where have you been, Gloria? I've been trying to contact you.'

'I'm so sorry, Horace.'

'And why are you calling me Horace?'

She felt rather sorry for him. Horace looked like the oldest teenager in the business, yet without a shadow of doubt he was pre-hippyite man. And there was an air of extinction about him. He was a fantastic example of Burberry man, in his brown corduroy suit that had been made before God created the world and would last long after post-Burberry man had destroyed it.

'Come on, tell me my name.'

'Oh you are courageous, standing behind your genuine tortoiseshell glasses.' She drained down her second pink gin, and now felt on top of the world.

'Where have you been, Gloria? I really have been trying to get hold of you.'

'Many men, darling, have been trying to get hold of me. Now, I know you may think this rather incredible, but I know I know you; but I don't know how I know you. Please don't laugh.'

He laughed, and ordered more of the same. 'Gloria, you are so utterly impossible, and you have the weirdest sense of humour. You never change.'

'Darling, I do apologize, but I do have these lapses.' She leaned towards him, simulating a loving kiss, but noticing he smelled of baked apples, she backed away.

'I merely happen to have published your book.'

So that's who he was.

'And for that I do apologize,' he continued. 'Not for publishing your book, but for publishing it rather badly. And at the wrong time. Incidentally, would you like to buy at reduced rate, one thousand five hundred copies that I happen to have had bound by mistake?'

'I purchased a plethora, remember?'

'Seriously, Gloria, I felt rather bad about it all. It should have been a best-seller.'

'Oliver. Oliver Meredith. You've suddenly dawned upon me.' This time she almost hugged him, but she did manage to touch his actual flesh with her actual lips.

He drew back from her. 'Where have you been, you naughty girl? I've been tinkling you for months. They wouldn't say where you were.'

She did not feel anger, just terribly sad. It was useless trying to explain to yet another face that she had been away for just a few weeks. The disease of forgetfulness seemed to be spreading its spores everywhere. It seemed useless fighting against it. The corner table became empty, so she navigated her way through the sea of lovely Bohemian people, and she sat herself down under a sepia photograph of a French boxer. 'Poor chap.'

He was obviously deceased. Some photographs communicated an aura of death. And quite suddenly she felt at peace with the whole world.

'So, where have you been?'

'Guess where?'

'Holloway Prison.'

'Darling, where else. No, actually I've been in Cannes with, guess who?'

'Aristotle Onassis.'

'He's far too impoverished for me, ducky. Actually, Pablo Picasso invited me to stay with him for a few weeks. So I did. Then I did more exciting things,' she winked and then spoke in a Walt-Disneyish French accent. 'Talking of lovairs, all those men in my memoirs, where are they? Not that my past was sordid. On the contrary, as you know it was beautiful and gay and astonishing. I would have thought one of them would have been driven by frenzy to sue me.'

But then again, perhaps it was just as well that the book was a failure and had passed the world like a deaf and dumb ship in the night. It was probabably to the good that the book had not become a best-seller, and that she had not suddenly been whisked into the limelight just for the sake of a cheap thrill for millions of morons to get their fix of vice. Because that's what they would have expected. But they would have been disappointed. And in the long run she was pleased that they had refrained from being cheated; she had hated the jacket and its blurb the moment she saw it. She now knew that she could not have coped with the success of the book. Anonymity was not necessarily nice, but at least you knew where you were. Success had too many drawbacks, she could see that now. She was glad that her previous prayers for success had not been answered by that nothing in the clouds.

'I'm so glad the book failed,' she said.

'I'm so sorry the book failed,' he said. He hadn't listened to her but seemed lost inside himself.

'Poor Oliver. What do they know? Who wants the truth?'

'But darling, it wasn't the truth. It was a wonderful concoction from out of your own fantastically camp mind.'

'But it was true, Oliver. Every amour, every face, every word. It was as true as us.'

'How true are we?'

She watched the pathetic creature dreaming; willingly wanting to barter his own puny existence for any other identity on earth.

'What happened to all your old lovers, Gloria?'

'They weren't that old.'

'I suppose they're all dead, or they would have sued.'

'None of them are dead. You just didn't distribute the book; nor get it well reviewed.'

'Oh Gloria, that imagination of yours.' He laughed.

Oliver would still not face up to her reality. She would not tell him again that every word of that book had been true. They had all existed, all those lovely men; and she had loved them all. Even those who had fallen through the memory hole. They were all her boys and she herself had been perfectly stupid not to have realized that some of them might have taken a terrible revenge upon her in the High Court, however nice they were, if they had suddenly become aware of exposure.

'If only someone would have sued us, Gloria, even someone who thought he recognized himself in your novel.'

20

'I will tell you for the last time. it was my autobiography.'

'Yes, Gloria, we all love you. We all love you very much. And you wrote a perfectly divine and strangely talented little book.'

The poor swine was demented. She felt rather sorry for him. To add to all his other problems, and they probably included latent homosexuality, he was also stark raving mad, but quietly, in a literary, Georgian fashion. Gloria suddenly felt rather ungay, and all around an aura of ungayness was spreading. The ungay hour was certainly descending upon the whole of Soho.

'Anyway, who cares,' he said, caring. 'Who cares about money?'

'Who cares about money. Only those with it and those without it,' Gloria replied. 'Incidentally, did I earn any?'

He laughed long, squeezing out the ridicule to the last bitter drop.

'Don't worry, Oliver, I don't need money.'

She noticed him looking down at her slightly faded Persian lamb that held her poor old singing bones together. 'I choose to wear this coat, Oliver. Incidentally, will you remind me to insert in my will that I will be buried only in this coat, with nothing on underneath.'

He hooted to try and levitate his spirit, but he failed. Then he took out a five-pound note and pressed it into her hand. 'Pay me back when you can afford it.'

He really believed that she was broke.

'Oliver, how many more times do I have to tell you, I don't need money.' But she did not give him back the fiver. Poor lamb, one needed to be generous these days; and it was very generous to take with good grace from someone who needed to give.

He had never taken her to where he slept nor to where he lived. But that was surely because he practically lived in pubs and offices. She was pleased that he had never taken her to the room that he must have had somewhere.

She could just imagine it. The socks scattered over the floor, stinking. The trousers inside out, the shirts hanging over the sink, only their collars soaking in cold water. And the stench of it all. Men were such beasts. 'Poor darlings.'

'Where you off to, Gloria?'

'Home. Where else?'

'I shall accompany you.'

She waited by the door as he started downstairs. 'Just having a little pee. Won't be a mo.'

When he returned he wrapped himself into his teddy-bear overcoat. 'How about one for the road?'

'Yes, one for the Charing Cross Road.'

She was pleased. For although she longed for her own bed, she could well afford putting off Edith and the boys for a little longer. But there was no avoiding the inevitable rendezvous. She was well aware of that. Being in that place had been all very well, but in the end it was no answer. Gloria had always known that in the end she would have to face up to things. One could not escape. There was no more running away, but in the meantime it was so nice to have a short holiday from the inevitable.

'Cheers,' he said, putting one arm around her.

Never, never had he once made the slightest suggestion. Never had his tiny finger stroked her in anything more than the purest affection. She was glad, but she wondered why. And boys were not his problem, as far as she knew. The only thing Oliver seemed addicted to was being an unsuccessful publisher. They downed their drinks and suddenly and quickly they re-entered the street without speaking.

Walking back towards Seven Dials she wondered whether her home would still be there. For although Rome wasn't built in one day, Hiroshima did disappear in less than one night. But she soon dismissed these thoughts as irrational, and exorcising the cataclysm from her mind, she decided to see Shorts Gardens and Neal Street standing exactly as they had done ever since the plague. And already her nostrils were assailed with the smells of rotting oranges and onions and cabbages. The wonderful smells of Covent Garden. Gloria was almost home and there was just the question of crossing Charing Cross Road and negotiating just a few more friendly streets.

'You always say you don't need money, Gloria. You always claim you have so much more than you need.' Oliver turned away from her as he spoke. And surprisingly, he stared at a young, overpainted bird of paradise; the sort that lost their feathers around the age of nineteen and a half years old, and flew away pathetically on one wing, in the direction of Shell-Mex House, never to be seen again. However, his sexual leer was embroidered with a quizzical intellectual expression, so she forgave him. 'Oliver Meredith, you are an iconoclast.'

He returned to her and she was glad that his neck was no longer in danger of dislocation.

'Yes, I have said time and again, I always admitted quite openly, that I'm very well off. All my lovers were absolute poppets and I was terribly fortunate that each understood one of the basic facts of human existence upon this earth. The need for financial security.'

23

'Gloria, why don't you take a world trip? Or two world trips? If you can afford it. What are you saving your money for? You're not going to live for ever.' He was sending her up, but she had no desire to convince him that she wasn't poverty-stricken. Men seemed to get such fixed ideas.

She resisted the urge to slap him extremely hard around the chops and she hoped he wasn't clever enough to see the venom in her eyes. She composed herself. 'Mr Meredith, I'm saving up my money for a rainy day.' She was very pleased that he was such an unsuccessful publisher.

But suddenly she became aware of the weather and she wished that it hadn't been raining at that precise moment. She knew exactly how he would reply and she mimicked his words within her. 'But Gloria darling, that rainy day is here.'

She stopped for a moment to catch her reflection in the window of a bookshop. 'Rainy day indeed.' She knew she could not pass for early forty any more, but nobody, not even that inverted sentimentalist Oliver Meredith, could accuse her of looking anything like her age. It was the bone structure that did it. The high cheekbones sculpted by the genes of her ancestors, all the way into her father's past, through Normandy and across the plains of Europe, along the Danube basin, and possibly even as far as Outer Mongolia. And on her mother's side, down, down through the ages; down to the Iberian peninsula, through the Flamenco Celtic mists, back possibly to the lost continent of Mu. But certainly as far as Cordova. How many could boast such a lineage?

She moved away from the window when she realized it was a porn shop, but Oliver Meredith still stood glued to the glass, staring at the girly magazines with his hands hunched into his teddy-bear coat. He was pretending to be far away in thought and not nursing his obviously feeble erection. So she walked on without him and felt a certain compassion. Men seemed to have a need for such elementary stimulation. But she didn't look back at him, just in case he walked towards her like a cripple. But he had obviously done what he had to do, and he hurried to catch up with her.

'Hurry, Gloria, it's pissing down. Come in here.' He pushed her to where he pointed. The café she knew so well, the Come As You Are.

But before she entered the café she looked back across the road at the house. The house that stood almost exactly opposite. It was her house. Her home.

There was a light on. 'That silly bitch Edith! She does it on purpose.' Oliver didn't seem to understand what she was on about at all. 'Why does she waste my electricity? Even if it's dark, it's still day. Isn't it?' She searched his face for confirmation.

'Oh yes. It is daytime.'

'There you are. The stupid cow. I'll get her for this.'

The glow of the premature bulb made her feel sick inside. So she was pleased to leave the sickening and suddenly contracting street.

'Why, look who's here,' Oliver said.

Gloria looked, and saw that it wasn't good.

3

'James! Hello, I'd like to introduce you to Gloria Gaye.'

She remembered the journalist only too well. A nothing face like that was unforgettable. The hand came forward, and it was as limp as a rotten cucumber. Gloria had always avoided any sort of contact with this sort of man in the past. Soho was like that. All sorts of wheels could revolve without impinging upon one another.

The face opened its mouth to mutter, and emitted so much alcohol gas into the air that you could have exploded the whole café with one match. But she was not kinky in that particular way, so she manufactured a smile. 'Yes, we have met,' he said.

'Really, I don't remember,' she replied.

Then they started conversing about a subject most drear to her heart. The book again. There was no avoiding it. She wished she had not allowed herself to be talked into publishing that book. It was probably true that everyone kept a diary at some time or other. Every little squirmy virgin probably put pen to paper as soon as her little boobs started blooming. But externalizing one's sexual fantasies in one's own private diary was a far cry from allowing the whole world to read over your shoulder. So she had only herself to blame.

'Did I write about it?' The words of James stumbled drunkenly out of him.

'No dear boy, but perhaps there's still time.'

'If there was an angle,' he said, 'I'd be only too pleased.'

'No thank you, let sleeping bitches lie.'

Suddenly the whole café laughed. It seemed that everyone had heard her and was hungry for enjoyment. The two painted queers, for instance, at the next table; they laughed so much she thought they would be sick.

'You may be a bitch, Gloria darling, but you never lie.'

'Actually I am not a bitch and I lie all the time.'

But the journalist was not amused. He was as deep in thought as he could be.

She looked under the table at his shoes. You could always tell a man's bank balance by the state of his footwear. And James obviously had a huge overdraft. On top of that, he either couldn't afford razor blades, or was attempting to grow a beard. So either way he was not to be trusted.

'Well, can you resurrect the book?'

She hated the way Oliver was pleading.

'Can't you think of some angle?'

'I would like to help you, Oliver. Let's see what I can do.' He was thinking again. It was most dangerous, but she didn't feel entirely ready to cross the road and go inside. Not yet. In a few more minutes she would be up to it without a doubt.

'Tell him where you've been, Gloria. Go on, trust him. I'm sure one nice story would do the trick and God knows, I need it.'

Everyone needed it, somehow or other. She knew she needed something, though what it was she couldn't imagine. She certainly needed the café not to start hurtling down through endless space. And she certainly needed not to have been followed by unseen feet or eyes to her own door. Soon she would make a dash for it and then she would be safe. She needed her own bed. And possibly she needed a real trip to Madeira or Cannes or the Dolomites.

When she opened her eyes again, she saw that the street outside was dead. And the houses that huddled around her house were dead. They were still there, but they were dead. They were empty of people and of furnishings. No lights were on and there were no curtains, and they were all boarded up. And there were words chalked upon the planks of wood. 'Lot 59', 'Lot 61'. She felt like Lot's wife, and did not even wish to question the horrible thing that would irrevocably follow if she did not look away.

'Please Gloria, all we need is one little angle. Tell him where you've been. It may be irrelevant to you but it could be a godsend. Please, we need it, we need it.'

'Please Oliver, the book is dead. Let it rest in peace.' She felt sorry for him, he had no one, not even himself.

'If I remember rightly, the novel was very well received,' James drooled.

'It was not a novel and it was not received. It shook no hands with Royalty. Don't you dare call it a novel, I won't have it. Please leave me alone. The book is dead, dead and buried. I paid the price, now leave it and me alone.' She inhaled the steam from her coffee and the mouths and eyes of the men opposite fell silent.

Gloria did not care for a resurrection, for a resurrection would only lead to another crucifixion.

Adrian the café owner came out of the back room where he had been making more of his walnut and gherkin sandwiches. He talked to himself above the till for a moment, then he beamed across to her all his undying adoration. 'Gloria my love! How lovely to see you again,' he said, ever so softly.

She loved Adrian and that reassuring smell of Miss Dior that went with her. 'Him?'

'Adrian,' Gloria said. She was so pleased to see the sad, gay face again.

'Where have you been, Gloria? Somewhere lovely?' Adrian mouthed secretively, in the style of one woman in a crowded room, asking another woman about the advent of the curse or the full sordid details of hysterectomy.

'What are they doing to the street outside?' Oliver had just noticed the deserted film set of Shorts Gardens. 'Are they rebuilding out there? But isn't that your house, Gloria?'

She didn't reply.

'Anyway, it can do with rebuilding.'

'Ducky, it doesn't need rebuilding, it needs pulling down.'

Her reply caused them all to titter, but she hoped that the powers that be would not think she was concurring with any possible decision that they had already imposed upon her world. So she crossed her fingers and her legs and her eyes, for a moment. If they pulled her street down, and her house down, they would pull her down also. And no one, not even Holborn Borough Council, could be that heartless.

But James the limp Jameson-filled journalist was still going on. 'But let's do try to think of some angle. It's up to you of course, but let's see what—'

'Shut your ugly little mouth,' she heard herself say. But he did not wipe the smile off his face.

'I've already paid the price, I lived for the day when that book came out. But when it did, I wanted to disappear. I wanted to be anonymous, and I still do. Oliver! Tell your *friend* to go, just go. Get out of my eyes.'

Adrian waved. She waved back. The two men opposite stood up. Oliver bent towards her and kissed her on the cheek. 'I'll tinkle you.' He left the café, and James followed him, walking backwards to the door like someone who had seen *High Noon*. And when they were gone, she dismissed them and now she felt very happy again. Now it would be quite easy to enter her house. Soon.

When she looked out of the window again, she saw the two men walking away, down the street. They were like conspirators. And beyond them were the hoardings, the empty houses, the dead street. And the lone lighted window of Edith's, inside her bricks. She hated that sickening heavy feeling within her lower stomach and wanted to go to the lavatory and excrete it out of herself. But she didn't move, she just wanted to be anonymous.

Adrian was nice, he would not mention the book nor the failure of the book. She had given him a signed copy, she remembered, and the next day he told her that his mascara had been running all night. But dear Adrian had not mentioned it since. He had the grace to let it die in peace.

Gloria now only wanted to curl up inside herself; to drink some more coffee and to chat with Adrian, just that. And then she would go home.

Adrian indicated that he would join her just as soon as he finished whispering to an obvious rough trade tearaway in the far corner. The man who was hiding behind the scar on his cheek.

She was glad that the book had not been successful. And she was not rationalizing the failure. She had never been in the market for giving herself an easy time. She had not wanted success, yet when it didn't come, she admitted she was unhappy. Gloria was quite prepared to accept all the manifold contradictions within herself. She adored her complexities as much as she adored Adrian and loathed Edith. She had spent herself upon herself; she had paid the price for her passionate past. She was buried and it was buried. True there would be another crucifixion sooner or later, but at this precise moment she was being born again and she could forget the past. She was being born again, here and now, and she could start from here. She could start all over again from where she was.

Adrian floated across towards her, his perfume arriving just slightly ahead of him.

But out of the corner of her eye she saw a figure in the street. It darted into a desolate doorway and she wondered who it was. She had hoped she had given him, whoever he was, the slip. That same old figure from the past who invariably followed her, and never fully revealed himself. She had sometimes caught a glimpse of the face, that familiar unknown face, that indelible face whose name was on the tip of her tongue. That face appeared as often as her recurring dream, that recollection that she could fly. Outside was the face that she was flying away from, yet she did not fear him immensely and sometimes she even longed for him to catch her, no matter what he wanted her for. And often she chided herself for fearing him and running away. One day she knew that she would come face to face with him. And the funniest thing of all; she knew that when that time came, she would embrace him.

But meanwhile, she had to face living in the world of reality and the smiling face of Adrian looming above her.

4

She couldn't take the face. The smile was broadening out into an expression of bestiality.

'Gloria, at last we can have some chat,' it said.

She had to get away from the face of Adrian that hovered above her. He was changing into a parrot or an owl or eagle. If she did not move sharpish, he would drive his beak into her eyes and turn her sight all red.

'Goodbye, Adrian.'

'Oh dear.' Of course it was disappointed. It had been done out of its prey. Friends were too much to bear these days. At least you knew where you were with your enemies. She longed for Edith, for the sanctuary of enmity.

'Toodle-oo anyway, poppet. See you soon,' he squeaked.

She waved with one hand whilst the other covered her face, to protect it, and she hurried out of the café.

The world was in a sorry state indeed, when people following their inner natures were changing back into animals.

'Someone walked over my grave,' she said as she turned to face her house. She hated herself as she walked across the road. But she kept her head high. She was out of her mind of course, to go amongst the slime and filth; destructive and degrading filth. Filth stuck where it touched. If you put your finger in faeces, your whole hand turned brown. And your whole body, and you, stank, and they threw you away.

She fumbled in her crocodile bag for the key that she had not used for a few weeks. 'Well, all right, possibly it was a month and a few days.' Then she held it within her fingers; the key to the door. And she stood before her tower of bricks to say one last prayer for all the wretched inhabitants of the world without her walls. And she decided to forgive them all, in their elementary hells. And quite suddenly she decided to let herself off the hook.

If one had compassion for other people, why couldn't one have compassion for oneself? Everyone was going around pitying other people; why did they not take pity upon themselves for a change? If you could only do this you could live with yourself, and come to terms with yourself; with what you were, and are, and could be. And what you could not be.

'He said, "Love thy neighbour as thyself," AS THY-SELF! Surely the Christians had got it all wrong. They stress the love thy neighbour bit, but not the as thyself bit.' Gloria decided there and then to have more compassion for herself in the future.

She slid the key into the slot, looked over her shoulder at the barricaded street to see if the figure would now have the guts to reveal himself, and declare his intention. But as usual, no one was there and she felt glad and strangely, slightly sad. So she turned to face her future. When she had gone through this door before, it had been the other way around; it had been to retreat from the nasty realities that had been forced upon her by the stillbirth of the book.

'Why was I controlled by such uncontrollable desires

33

to kill myself?' she said, and entered the house.

Her stairs opened up like a lover's arms before her. She had no wish to kill herself now, on the contrary, she had all her life in front of her; besides, she wasn't the dying sort.

'Tutankhamen!' she called. 'Tutankhamen!' But there was no miaow, no avalanche of fluffy blue candy-floss rushing towards her. But that was no reason to stop smiling.

'Edith! Edith!'

Then she heard her coughing in her room. It was a wet disgusting sound. Gloria looked at her watch and wondered why it was so dark, so early. And she also wondered why Edith was not at work. Nothing had ever kept Edith from work, which apparently was so vital to the survival of the nation. How could the Ministry of Agriculture and Fisheries survive without the match-stick virgin within its walls? How could the Common-wealth hold together and not fall into chaos without Edith Ramsey, M.B.E. or O.B.E. (or so she claimed), there at the helm?

'Or was is it O.T.F.F.? The Order of the Frozen Fanny.' She laughed, then rapped upon the door. 'Edith!'

The autumnal voice croaked from within, 'Oh do enter.'

Gloria prided herself that she wasn't like most land-ladies, who barged into the rooms of their lodgers at any time of day or night, during any sort of awkward moment; not that Edith was ever likely to have an awkward moment.

And so she entered, and Edith lay stretched out before her, in a sort of do-it-yourself crucifixion.

'Oh, you've come back at last,' Edith gasped.

34

'Edith, why aren't you at work? What's happened to the street? Where's everyone?'

'I'm not feeling very well, Gloria. And I've got all my packing to do.'

'Did you hear me, why are all the houses empty? Where have all the people gone? What's happened?'

'Oh, I have the most frightful heartburn,' Edith moaned and moaned.

'Edith! Pull yourself together. And where's my beautiful Tutankhamen?'

'It's all your fault, Gloria. The Town Hall said they gave you—' she crumbled into silence.

It was always the same. You just had to turn your back for five minutes and everything went haywire. One couldn't even afford to blink these days, without causing some kind of cataclysm. But on the other hand, you could rely upon Edith, she had not changed. She was just as stupid and hopeless as she had ever been, and as usual she was bitching about something or other to cover up the sound of her death rattle.

'The man from the Town Hall said you were notified, a year ago, and six months ago. He came in person. And they wrote to you several times warning you—informing you about the deadline.' She fluttered her eyelids like Mimi, and subsided into silence again.

'Deadline? Edith, stop going on. Stop talking a lot of tosh and tell me where my Tuti is.'

'Yes. It's a compulsory purchase and they've all gone, everyone from the street—for the widening. And the man from the Town Hall said you were offered a lovely house in Wanstead or in Walthamstow. And compensation. But you just wouldn't listen, but now you'll have to. Now you're in a right pickle and I must pack my things.'

Perhaps this time she really was gasping her last; for as nutty as she was, Edith had never been this incoherent.

Gloria looked around the room. Nothing seemed to be missing; so far. Edith had not sold any of the furniture. She went to the door and opened it. 'Here, pussy, pussy, pussy. Where are you, Tutankhamen? Where are you, sweety puss?'

'Please close the door, the draught will finish me off.'

Gloria complied. 'Now what's all this about? Please, Edith, come back to earth for once in your life and tell me what it's all about.'

Edith stood up and it was such a beautifully fraught performance, Gloria wanted to applaud.

'You know perfectly well that you don't want to face up to it, Gloria. But now you will have to.' She put the kettle on.

'I shall face what I choose to face.'

'No, Miss Gloria Gaye, you can't get away from this one,' she said vindictively, but then immediately went all genteel. 'Would you like a nice cup of tea?'

'Yes please, two sugars.'

'It's all coming down, and about time too.'

'Oh, it's all been coming down ever since I can remember. This house, this entire street was condemned before the First World War. But I dare say, by the way things look, it will last longer than the world. They've been going on about this for years, take no notice, Edith dear. But where is that cat?'

Edith handed her a cup of tea.

'Thank you, you are a poppet.' Whatever happened, there would always be a cup of tea. When the end of the world was announced there would be two English
36

ladies in a room somewhere, dissolving four cubes of sugar with two teaspoons.

'You see, Gloria, you never face things, but you must. The whole street has moved out. And you must go. You've always imagined that you are above the law, that the rules never apply to you. I tried to contact you in that place, time and time again—'

So, all those phone calls had been from Edith. It was just as well she hadn't gone to the kiosk. When people wanted you on the phone it was nearly always for them, and never for you. It was always to their advantage.

'—it's the widening you see. Who are we to hold up progress? Everyone's been rehoused, and very nicely. I believe. And compensated.'

'Edith, you're repeating yourself.'

'And some horrible official-looking men came in plain clothes, asking for you. Why didn't you keep in contact with me? And the boys have gone, and I'm going tomorrow, because the deadline was yesterday and you must start packing because you simply won't be allowed to stay. This house will be as flat as a pancake next week.'

What was she going on about? Her two darling boys could not have gone; they wouldn't want to live away from her. Besides, what other landlady could possibly stand the noise of two queer contortionists who seemed to practise only at night? But she was worried about her Tutankhamen. With all the noise and all the goings on, he was probably hiding in some terrible corner somewhere, afraid to come out. The poor darling. What did the world care about cats? For highly sensitive, highly rare pussy cats.

'Edith, I think you need a sedative.'

The woman came up to her, and had the audacity to clutch her wrists with those horrible bony fingers. But she seemed to have more strength in her leathery carcass than one could possibly have imagined.

'Gloria, if you don't go, they will evict you. You must leave now. Tonight. Or they'll prosecute.'

'They've been persecuting me for years, I will hear no more of it. Anyway, even if you haven't dreamed this up, do you imagine that I will move from here? Do you think I could continue this existence away from my home? It would be like losing my body. Calm down and stop being hysterical.'

The woman relaxed her grip, and sipped noisily from her cup of tea. Then she stood on a chair and pulled down an empty suitcase from the top of the wardrobe.

Gloria looked in amazement at the frantic way Edith's eyes darted around the room, and the panicky way she started to pack her sickly pink undies and her long skirts. Those skirts had been built a long time ago, but the wheel had come full circle and they were in fashion again. Well, almost.

And even if it was true that the street was going to be pulverized, and flattened out of existence, was that any reason to panic? 'Let everyone else in the world panic. Gloria Gaye does not give in to petty bureaucracy.'

In the end, the individual who had the courage to hold out would win through. There were still some decent people left in the world, people who took up the lost causes of the undaunted. It was a sort of vicariousness, just like cheering on the Christian in the arena against the lions.

Her house would not be torn to pieces. She would stand alone, and her house would stand alone, amongst
38

all the devastation, if need be. 'They reckoned without me, Edith.' She spoke quietly.

But Edith just shook her head, and now she was whimpering.

'And what about my boys? I don't believe you. You said they had left me. I don't believe you.'

But now Edith was crying full blast. Tears were running down her cavernous face and along her scrawny neck. 'You must go. You must go. You must carry out their instructions. We must leave immediately.'

'They'll have to carry me out.' Gloria laughed a lot to shut out the sound of the hysterically lamenting and packing Edith.

She cast her mind back to those weeks, just before she had gone to Belton. Yes, she did remember a mongolfaced official. He burbled on at the door about some ridiculous scheme or other. She had opened that first letter. Yes, it was all coming back to her now. She had read the nonsense it contained. But thereafter she never bothered to open any more of those sickening official paid envelopes. She just scrunched them up into a ball and let her darling pussy cat chase them all over the house. He loved that, Tutankhamen.

'Anyway, enough of that. All I want to do now is find him. There's plenty to do in life without worrying about the sort of people who make life painful.' She had done the only thing possible; the only way you could win with them was to appear not to fight, but to retreat quietly and bide your time, and only meet them head on when you were ready. The aura of depression that had suddenly descended upon the house was not due to the impending battle; for on this score she had no doubt whatsoever that she would win a resounding victory. The clammy feeling of dread was rather due to the absence of the cat.

Edith had already filled one case, and now she lay upon the bed before embarking upon another. Her body was turned to the wall; she looked like a long sack of bones.

Gloria left the room but left the door open. 'Where is that stupid cat? Tutankhamen!' she called, and called again.

'He's ... dead,' Edith said, following her out into the passage.

'Don't you dare! How dare you say such a terrible thing. Tutankhamen dead! You wicked hag. I won't hear of it.'

'At least I think he's dead. He ran away a few weeks back and it's common knowledge he's dead.'

'Very common,' Gloria snarled at her lodger, and walked away.

That cat was more alive than any human being she had ever met. Except, of course, Mr Moss. Edith adored doing things like that. That cat had many more lives to live, yet. And although it was true he had used up nine lives two times over, he was now embarked upon another series of lives, and there could be no doubt that he was in some corner just sleeping away, not knowing that the long night was over. His mistress had come home, and there would be liver and lights and mackerel, and Jersey milk, forever.

Gloria entered her living-room and breathed it in. She just stood still and bathed within the smell of it. And before she did anything else she switched on the record player, and the music of Gershwin once more entered her soul. 'George,' she said. 'Dear George.'

Gloria danced. And she removed her coat, her hat,

and scarf. It all became part of the choreography. 'Some day he'll come along, the man I love. And he'll be big and strong, the man I love...'

It was good to get away from Edith's room because it stank of her and she stank of the Ministry of Agriculture and Fisheries.

Gloria was feeling much, much better and she decided to take one of those miraculous tablets from the little bottle they had given her when she left the hospital. 'Oblivdexital,' she remembered the name as she popped one in her mouth. They really worked. They really stopped rooms tilting up and revolving, they really stopped furniture from attacking you. Just one tiny tablet kept people quite human, and stopped them changing into predatory animals. Science was a wonderful thing.

She slumped into her favourite armchair and gazed around at every beautiful item she had bought out of the obscure markets of Waterloo and Camberwell and Dalston and Islington. Her precious belongings, her statuettes of Hanuman and Shiva. Her divine bronze Gautama, and her copper turtle; and her oils. Those peaceful Victorian landscapes of fields and rivers and church spires, and her reproductions of Rubens, and Toulouse-Lautrec. There was nothing else upon this earth more fantastic, more necessary, than coming home.

The effects of the pill were immediate and she felt quite blissful as she floated into herself. From her toes to the top of her forehead, gradually peace was flowing right through her.

'Peace is around me, within me, above me, beneath me ... I am peace, I live in piss.' She admired her own, rather nice sarcasm. It was pretty obvious that there was something wrong with the world, it was all the piss, all around. The unkind poison, the pus of sad people. And it suddenly dawned upon her, that essential factor that had eluded her in the past. It was not good to take pills in order to relax, but once one was relaxed, then one could quite easily afford to take them.

It was never too late to learn. Far from it, she had all the time in the world, and all the fight, and all the courage in the world.

She would not disintegrate, she would not fall apart. And Mr Moss was bound to come and he would help her solve all her outstanding problems. And possibly she would go away with him. Meanwhile she allowed herself the blissful luxury of dozing off and closing down the world.

5

'Ramona, I hear the mission bells above, Ramona,
they're ringing out—'

That was nice, she had dropped off and had been
singing the lovely song within her dream; and she
woke singing, '—I press you, caress you—'

But that terrible woman had entered and ruined
everything.

'I do not understand you at all. You know that we
shouldn't be here, yet you lie there, singing. Can't you
see? Your darling boys have gone, and you won't accept
it. Tutankhamen's probably dead, and you just won't
take it in. Gloria, come down to earth and pull yourself
together.'

'If you're pulled together, I'm glad I've been let
out.'

'—I press you, caress you,' she continued singing.
Maybe if she just ignored the woman, she would
disappear.

'You worry too much, Edith, but then, you always were
a frightful worrier.' She toyed with a curved Moorish
dagger, fingering the mother-of-pearl that had been so
delicately set in the wooden handle. It took her back
to the Minza in Tangier, with those magnificent carpets,
and the pouffes, and the poofs, and that mad Arab
hashish smuggler who was only too normal. He certainly

went down in her estimation when he went down in his magnificent yacht.

It would have been quite nice to plunge the dagger into Edith's eyes. They were so dead. She would have been far more interesting spouting fountains of blood out of each eyeball.

Gloria leaned over for the Drambuie instead. 'Have a drink, Edith darling. There's some South African sherry on top of the piano. Maybe you'll play it while you're there.'

She saw Edith's look of amazement and didn't wonder. She had always been far too kind to the wretched woman. But one had to try to spread happiness in this dark world, no matter how thinly one had to spread one's resources.

'I adore you when you're nice, Gloria.' Edith ruffed up her sleeves and poised her bones above the ivory keys.

'Pale hands I love, beside the Shalimar—' Edith sang in her frail fruity soprano. Gloria decided to make the sound more bearable so she joined in with her own amber contralto, eventually closing her ears to the horrifying warble of the woman from the Ministry of Agriculture and Fisheries.

She would be doing her a favour; putting her out of her agony with such a beautiful blade, but who would believe that the act was one of pure altruism?

The stain from Edith's off-white blood would not be too difficult to remove from the carpet. Yet she quite liked Edith, and although she wanted to see the back of her, there were many worse people in the world. Though she had been extremely lucky so far, and had not met any of them.

'Hey Edith, remember that fabulous time when we

44

were in that marvellous show together? Wasn't it called the Sugar Babies of Brighton? Or something? You know, when I had that solo part with the golden umbrella.'

'Yes, I do remember. But you only lasted a few weeks. You had only just joined the Merry Throng, and you upped and got married.'

'Please, I don't want to talk about that. I loved the theatre. I would have given many more years to it, but five or six years were all I could spare.'

Edith had the audacity to gasp. 'But, Gloria, you were only in that show for three weeks—'

'Shut up! Do you hear me?'

'Your entire career lasted exactly three months, if you string all those jobs together.'

She knew she would not be able to contain her wrath. Edith would get hers, eventually. Meanwhile Gloria sat upon her hands; just in case.

'You are a ruthless calculating liar. Or perhaps I ought to be kind and say it's merely senile decay of the brain cells. You know full well how many years of my life I donated to the theatre. So shut your filthy mouth or I shall shut it for you.'

She shut it. Gloria tittered and then smiled. Unfortunate creatures needed sympathy.

'I'm sorry, Gloria, I don't want to upset you.' Edith had such a shrill voice, she would be doing her a favour by catapulting her into eternity. And perhaps strangulation would be the best means of propulsion.

'Come on, Edith, get your coat on, I'm taking you out.'

Gloria looked at the woman who was still tickling the piano keyboard. Edith hadn't absorbed the impact of her invitation.

45

'Yes, I do remember Sugar Babies, Gloria. You looked so nifty in those days. We were very naughty.'

'We were never naughty, we were merely frisky. But I say, Edith, do you remember Budapest and Istanbul? My bottom still bears the scars. It's the city of black and blue bums.'

'We never went ... I don't think I ever ...'

'What? What did you say?'

'Nothing, I must continue my packing.'

'What's happened to your mind, Edith? Surely you remember? It was there that I suddenly started to shoot up and up. Remember how I exploded in that show? Pour me another Drambuie, there's a love. Remember how I lit everyone up with my magic phosphorus over the Bosphorus?'

Edith shook her vacant head very slowly. 'I'm sorry, Gloria, I don't remember.'

'Edith, I despair. How the hell do you think I accumulated all these beautiful things?' Her hands and arms conducted the beautiful symphony of her room. There was nothing else you could do with Edith. What was there to do with a person who destroyed the reality of her past?

But the stupid bitch would not shut up. 'All this life of yours, Gloria, is fantasy. I'm worried for you. I don't like leaving you. What about your daughter, let me phone her.'

'Stay away from that phone or I'll throttle you. I'll throw you out if you go on like this.'

She herself rushed to the telephone.

'You can't throw me out because I'm packing. You can't even throw yourself out, because it's too late.'

Gloria dialled Belton. The bloody place was engaged. It was always engaged. Someone was forever talking to

46

anyone about nothing. She dialled again and then slammed the receiver down.

She did not feel like throttling Edith just then. One could only feel sorry for a person who could die without leaving a solitary trace of herself behind. And no one would enquire about her. No one would weep one solitary tear for her.

'Then how did I get my money? How?' she said, despite herself. 'How did I do it without my lovers?' She wished that she wouldn't lose control of herself like this. How tedious it was to lack self-discipline. So she lowered her voice. 'How do I have all this security?'

'Don't let's go into that again. You know as well as I do, that all this talk of a fabulous past is sheer fantasy. And that includes your lovers.'

'Oh, then how did I get this house, which cost me ten thousand pounds ten years ago?'

'Your—now, don't fly off the handle—but you know perfectly well that your husband left you the money.'

'I had no husband, I was never married. Never. Never really. And who said he left me money when he died? He never died. He never lived. Where are you going? Come back.'

'I'm packing, remember? I'm going to Carshalton tomorrow morning. To Prissy.'

Gloria watched herself and Edith in the long mirror. They were a stupid pair of cows, haranguing each other like that; especially when they had been together ever since she had bought the house. Edith had been her first lodger and she paid her rent like clockwork, which was not surprising really, because she was operated by clockwork.

Gloria decided to calm herself down. If Edith had no self-control, there was no reason for her to act in the same way. 'Come on, you're coming out with me; I'm treating you.'

She walked over to the trembling creature. 'Come on, come on, let's bury this madness; let's whoop it up.'

'I hardly like going out these days. One just isn't safe in the streets. Men are such beasts.'

'You should be so lucky.' Gloria poked Edith in the ribs and they both laughed. Edith started hesitant and slow, but she soon caught on; becoming totally infected with gaiety.

'Where are we going?'

'I'll take you to the pictures. It's ages since I went to the flicks.'

Edith started to melt into a human being, but then: 'Oh, but—I've got my packing to do. We must—I must leave first thing in the morning.'

'Pack tomorrow morning then, there's always time. You always have time for your own funeral. Run along now, put on something warm.'

'Oh Gloria, I adore you; you're too kind to me.'

'I know.'

Edith skipped towards her room, and Gloria sighed and yawned, and stretched and danced; and went to the telephone and dialled that place again.

'Could you please ask Mr Moss to come to the phone. Mr David Moss. M O S S, S as in sleep.'

That imbecile porter at the other end of the line needed treatment himself.

'All right then, would you please give him a message. Tell him I shall be going out for a few hours, so he's not to phone me before eleven o'clock tonight. But he can phone, or just turn up, any time after that. Tell him I'm expecting him. Thank you,' she cooed and gently replaced the receiver. 'Idiot!'

48

Gloria left the room and walked down to where Edith was waiting for her with enough apprehension as you would need for an expedition into darkest Brazil. They descended and left the house and entered the world and walked towards the glow in the sky. It was not a forest fire, but merely neon.

'Oh Gloria, what's happened to England?'

'Edith, count your blessings, England may not be the best country to live in, but it's still the best country to sleep in.' She looked around at the weird inhabitants of the maze. 'Mind you, I'm not so sure there'll be any sleep for anyone, from now on.'

Gloria slipped another Oblivdexital into her mouth. It didn't go down at once, but lodged at the back of her throat for a while. But one could put up with the bitter taste, if it meant experiencing that beautiful inner calm that she needed as much as her next breath. There was always a price to pay, and this price she paid willingly. For the tablet had struck like lightning and she was floating along beside her friend; a blissful six inches above the paving stones of Leicester Square.

'I do hope Mr Moss gets my message. I wish he'd come soon. Incidentally, is it tomorrow yet?'

Edith always looked at her so weirdly. 'I mean, the sky looks so bright; it could easily be midnight and galloping towards the dawn. I do wish it is tomorrow. Mr Moss will certainly come then.'

'Who is Mr Moss?'

'Mr Moss is Mr Moss.' It was either foggy or there was a fire somewhere; a fire without smell. She walked towards the barrow. It was piled high with fruit from countries of sunshine. 'Maybe when Mr Moss comes he'll take me to Lyme Regis or Bournemouth. It would be nice to be high up and overlooking the ocean. And I'll never come back.'

'Yes lady?' the street trader said.

She was about to prod a beautiful bunch of big black grapes. The trader pointed to the printed message stuck amongst the fruit. It reprimanded her. 'DON'T SQUEEZE ME UNTIL I'M YOURS.'

'Frightfully sorry. Can I have that lovely bunch of cancer grapes, please?'

He was such a dear soul, taking it all in his stride. He just laughed as he weighed them, and he wrapped them and she counted out the money and paid for them. And they walked away.

'What did you mean? Cancer grapes?' Edith looked frightfully frail. Gloria hoped she would last the night out.

'They're the sort of grapes too good to eat. The sort you take to dying relatives, to decorate their death bed,' she replied. Her answer seemed to satisfy Edith, who now grasped her arm very tightly, and they entered the throng of gawpers massed outside the cluster of picture palaces.

'Where are you taking me?' Edith looked quite on edge.

'Yours is not to reason why. Just follow me into the romantic flickering dark, before you die.' She laughed in the foyer but Edith hadn't seen the joke. Rather she looked as if she were concentrating upon her last rites.

Gloria wondered why she had taken the loathsome bitch out with her.

'Maggots!' she said.

Edith responded. 'Why maggots?' But then her puzzlement subsided as she took in the compressed waiting faces surrounding her. Poor dear. Gloria hadn't the heart to tell her companion that she had suddenly felt a tremendous compassion for the maggots who would soon feed upon her.

'Isn't life gay, Edith? Isn't life beautiful?'

She propelled Edith towards an opening in the grey sea. It was marvellous to be out of that mental home; and to be over the manic and the melancholy of menopause, of those years ago.

'I've got the tickets, let's go inside.' She held the bony fingers of her friend and entered into the dark. It was so reassuring.

6

To breathe the night air, however foul, was certainly a relief after being in the bowels of that cinematic hell. And it was a pleasure just to stand there in the foyer, waiting for the mass of faces to clear. Then they moved towards the exit.

'What did you think of the picture, Edith?'

But Edith wasn't thinking, she seemed so far away and trying so desperately to follow her feet home to bed.

'It was about nothing. And it was acted by nonentities.'

'It got wonderful reviews—I—thought—it rather—interesting.' Edith replied between a bout of genteelly suppressed sneezes. 'Oh, now I've got the 'flu and I want to be well to travel.' She clutched at Gloria's arm and whined on. 'Oh dear, why did you have to choose tonight of all nights to take me out?'

'Whatever happens, you'll blame it on me. If you die, you'll blame it on me.'

They stood still outside the cinema for a moment. The cold night air slapped Gloria right on the face and she hoped that she wouldn't faint. And because she found it so hard to move away, she studied the stills and wondered why she always found it so hard now to travel anywhere. It had been like this for some time, each interior was merely an oasis in the dark world around; a stepping stone between dark and dark. Belton

Psychiatric Hospital, despite all its miracles, had not eliminated every one of her problems. But that was probably asking for too much.

'I thought it was a terrible film. A disgusting, nasty piece of work. There was no story, no characterization. In my day, at least you could hear what they were saying to each other. You knew who were the girls and who were the boys. Today, the only way you can tell their sex, is by who gets on top of who; and even then you can't be too sure. Women wanting to be like men! Men wanting to be like little boys! And everyone grunting, with sweaty armpits. And all those four-letter words, there's only one that's worth anything.'

'What's that?' Edith was trying to pull her away in the direction of home.

'Love. L O V E. Do you remember that word? Oh Edith, I'm very afraid...'

'So am I. I think I'm getting 'flu. I shan't be able to leave tomorrow and I shall be breaking the law by staying. I've never broken the law in my life.'

Edith was now looking very green around the gills. Or possibly it was the neon.

'You look as if you need some fuel, Edith. Come, let me buy you a steak.'

In a huge smokey window, a black boy in a tall white hat was sizzling slices of meat on a hot-plate. Gloria wondered why he was smiling and singing so happily to himself. He was bound to suffer for it all later, no one could be that happy and get away with it. Nevertheless, it was nice, and his face was like a white lotus upon an inky sea.

Edith held her hand to her rib cage and looked extremely in extremis, as she tried so hard to fight back the sneezes. 'Poor Edith.' No one would weep for Edith

53

when she expired. Perhaps some decrepit third cousin would put some horrible pink tulips on her grave; a bunch for four and sixpence. And they would lie there rotting, until the wind of a few winters hence blew the dried-up remains away, and Edith would be gone, forever. And she never would have existed.

'Yes, let me buy you a nice big juicy steak.'

'I want to go home to bed.'

'Incidentally, you never gave me the rent. You haven't spent it, have you? On a mini skirt, or something?'

Edith uncurled herself and she stood irate and upright; all six feet of her, which rather surprised Gloria. Recently Edith had been no more than four and a half feet tall. It had always been as if she was not on speaking terms with the sky, and wanted so much to communicate with her impending destination, that she stooped more and more towards it. There had been many an occasion when Gloria had to resist the urge of folding up the lady, completely in half, and packing her away in a suitcase.

'The rent is waiting for you on the mantelpiece in my room. I put it there every week, religiously. How could you even think that I would spend it. I feel there's nothing worth living for when you treat me this way.'

The thought of the money warmed her, and she could not resist the sight and the smell of steak much longer. 'Come inside and at least die on a full stomach!'

'You certainly know how to hurt me, Gloria. I don't know how I like you so much when I hate you so much.'

'KALI SHIVA, KALI SHIVA, SHIVA SHIVA, KALI KALI.' It was a frightful sound.

Gloria turned and saw the four dirty teenage eunuchs,

in their long purple robes, and at their tail end there followed a blonde cross-eyed pimply girl with steel-rimmed National Health glasses on her nose. She held a frying pan in one hand, and she had two little bells on the other thumb and forefinger. As they came close, Gloria felt sorry for them, but they seemed happy enough. The girl tinkled the bells and the boys grunted their song.

'GOD CREATION, GODDESS CHAOS, HEAR US! HEAR US! KALI KALI. GIVE US MONEY, GRASS AND HONEY, GOOD BE-LIEVER, SHIVA SHIVA!'

She rather liked them; they were rather picturesque, even if they were pathetically dishevelled.

'Edith, loan me half a crown.'

'There are no half-crowns any longer.'

'You say the most stupid things. Give me a two-shilling bit then.'

'There are no shillings any more. Here's ten pence.'

Gloria dropped the florin into the girl's pan. 'There, that will buy you a nice bowl of rice.'

She waved, 'Good luck,' then she turned and pushed the protesting Edith into the steak restaurant. 'They may be dirty, but at least they are sincere.'

'I can't keep up with things, Gloria. London is so foreign-looking. I'll be better off out of it.'

'Don't worry sweetie, you won't have long to wait.'

She wondered what Mr Moss was doing at the moment, and noticed a telephone near the door. She would try to get through a little later. On the other hand, it was quite possible that he had already left and was on his way to her.

They ordered, and the food was in front of them too quickly. One had to be suspicious when the service was too efficient. On the other hand, it looked absolutely delicious, and she was glad to exorcise all her forebodings, for in spite of the plastic customers in this sterilized interior, she had to admit that the smell and the sight of the food were absolutely delicious.

'I couldn't touch a thing.' Edith's eyes were closed and she was shaking her head.

Of course she couldn't, tortoises were not noted for their stomach capacity. 'Oh do try a little, dear, it's very nourishing.'

Edith just shook her pained head very slowly, and then inclined downward towards her lap as if she were about to pray.

'So where are my boys then? On tour?'

'No. They're in London.'

'How marvellous, playing London at last. And why not? They deserve it. After all, they are the best contortionists in the business. Are they playing the Palladium?'

'Gloria, you don't understand. Times have changed. They're working for Domestics Unlimited as charladies. You must face up to things.'

'Isn't it lovely. I knew they'd make the London Palladium in the end. They certainly deserve a break. They worked hard enough for it,' she replied. 'Isn't it lovely to see a big thick steak.' The knife went through the meat like a skiff through water.

There was something wrong with her taste. It was possibly the tablets; but this did not depress her. There was always a price to pay, and the tablets had been very beneficial, so one had to put up with such minimal side effects. But it did all taste the same. She tried the potato in its jacket, the green beans, and the bread, but it all tasted exactly of nothing.

'Is it my imagination, or is this food tasteless?'

'Where have you been, Gloria? All food is tasteless nowadays. You're living in the past.'

'If only that were so.'

Music was playing but there was no orchestra. It was piped music and she minded it as much as the food. It was music with the sweat extracted out of it. 'In ten years time, no doubt, it will be perfectly acceptable. Isn't it odd how time makes things respectable?'

'It's ten years time already, Gloria. Already it's perfectly acceptable; and respectable.'

'For once in your life you're right, Edith.'

She decided not to eat any more, so she closed her knife and fork and decided to pay the bill without any fuss whatsoever.

A chink of coins caused her to turn, and there were the purpled four and the cross-eyed, pimply girl. She had been counting out coins and making little neat piles of them, there must have been almost twenty pounds and it made Gloria furious; especially because they were all tearing into the chunks of steak before them.

She could not hold herself back. 'I thought that you would be vegetarians. After all, you claimed in your songs that you followed the Eastern Religions.'

She was rather pleased with the way she was handling the situation; for not allowing the fury raging within to show itself.

'We are vegetarian, lady, 'cept on odd days, when there's an R in the month.' They all laughed.

'Oh, and what is your religion?' Edith asked with legitimate interest, so Gloria kicked her ankle, under the table, but not too brutally.

'It's the religion I invented, wanna join us?' A boy with bum-fluff had the audacity to wink.

57

'Here, someone's gave us a Hong Kong rupee, bloody nerve.' He chucked it across the restaurant. But nobody responded in the tight, packed, polished interior, they just munched with their tight little mouths.

'Seem to remember you. Didn't you give us something, lady?'

'Yes! And I'm going to give you something more.'

They seemed so happy, even when she stood up and started swiping them with Edith's umbrella; the smile never seemed to leave their faces as she hit them mercilessly. She was a windmill suddenly gone berserk.

Plates were flying, and coleslaw; and Edith screamed, and it was quite amazing how quickly one could cause such havoc if one so desired.

'Help!' A long-drawn cry came from Edith as she lay flat upon the floor. 'My umbrella. Save it, someone, she'll break my umbrella.'

'Take your hands off me.' She knew how to deal with Cypriot waiters, so she forced herself free and strode to the door, waving at the startled dead, and glad to see the crimson stains of blood upon the purple people. And Gloria felt desperately happy for the first time in weeks.

'She's gone mad! She's gone mad!' Edith shouted as she gladly imprisoned herself under her chair. 'Get the police! Get the police!' She screamed.

But in the main, no one stirred from their fixed positions of surprise, and Gloria walked out into the night air singing, 'KALI SHIVA, KALI SHIVA, SHIVA SHIVA, KALI KALI...'

7

Gloria awoke in the morning feeling on top of the world. So she did not put off the day, but jumped out of bed immediately and went to the bathroom. She stood on the scales, and because it was necessary to face reality, she took her hand away from over her eyes. 'Gloria, you've lost. I'm proud of you.'

And she knew that for the rest of the day she would be happy. Quickly she poured some water on her face and eased herself into her silver lamé trousers. And then there was the knocking on the door. At last he had come. On her way down, she squirted herself with Miss Dior.

James the journalist almost fell in when she opened.

There are some people you just hate for no rhyme or reason; James was not one of these. You could only feel sorry for a man who only truly existed during licensing hours. Possibly this was the reason she even allowed him to advance a few steps into her interior.

'Gloria.'

'Have we met?'

'Miss Gaye. Surely you remember? We met a few days ago in the Come As You Are. Oliver introduced us.'

'A few days ago? It was yesterday.'

'Then you do remember. I can assure you, Gloria, it was the day before yesterday, to be precise.'

She hated him talking. Apart from the timbre of his voice, there was the danger of explosion. The air was becoming so thick with his fumes, that all he had to do was to light a cigarette and they would all be blown to Kingdom-Come.

'I can assure you that I do not lose whole days just like that. And what do you want?'

'I think I may possibly be able to resurrect your book. If we could sit down, I'm sure we could think up some angle to get it all going again. I know there's a big story in it somewhere, I can feel it in my bones.' The rat had managed to advance into the corridor.

'I've got no wish to resurrect anything. Please go, my lover is a very jealous man, and he is just flying in from Budapest.'

She inched him back towards the door. Such people did not belong to houses, but to the streets.

'Miss Gaye, I can help you.'

'Dear boy, you can't even help yourself.'

'I can get you all over the front pages.'

'Just get out of my life. I am all full up with people. I have no vacancies.' She slammed the door, and sang as she went back upstairs. 'We'll gather lilacs in the spring again. And walk together down an English lane.'

She decided to go out, because it was such a lovely day outside. And although she loved her house, there was too much quiet around today. She peered out of the window and down at her street. Only the fishmonger was apparent; and the few odd cats lingering around his stall. She craned her neck, but Tutankhamen was not there.

'He's bound to turn up. He's a naughty boy and he likes his bit of Persian fluff, but he always returns.'

Gloria went back to her living-room, to prepare herself for the necessary ordeal of the day before her. She loved the ritual of the mirror, and was pleased that she could face her reflection.

It was true that there had been shadows and sadness in her past, but only Adam's mother lived a life without fault or blemish.

She had her health and her looks, and she was not exactly short of money; and her skin was beautifully pale.

She concentrated herself properly in creating a face able to cope with the winds of Seven Dials. Those seven streets that came together just around the corner from where she lived, near Covent Garden. She had never told a living soul that she chose a different street for every day of the week. She would wander along each street in turn and start the day that way. It was not a big thing to tell anyone; it was just that she could not bear anyone laughing at something so seemingly trivial, yet important to her. And she was at the hub of the start of every day. And each street was a spoke in the wheel leading right into the waking flesh of the city. And how they followed her, the hungry young men.

''Twas all over my jealousy.' She always needed to tango around the room. One always needed to take very seriously one's need to act stupidly; in order to accompany oneself out of loneliness. But she did wonder why they all found her so attractive, those young ones. 'Poor darlings. Poor obscene darlings. All they need is comfort.' She danced around the room, moving her arms so gracefully, trying to reach an exact balance between Martha Graham and Ram Gopal.

She just hoped that Mr Moss would come today, for she needed someone desperately. She had experienced a lot of love and she had loved, and she had hated and

61

had been hated; and she had learned to live with a lot of things, but she simply could not live alone with herself any longer. She could not take the alternating love and hate in the face staring out at her from inside the mirror. Those snapping expressions. It needed so much armour to defend against loneliness. So she was glad that Mr Moss was possibly just around the corner. He would come and hold her and it would not be dirty but beautiful and precious and passionate, and they would melt into each other. No, she was done with the pretty boys, with that same skull grinning through those pink chubby faces; those horrible young creatures who were never tempered by experience, who had it all made for them because they were pretty. Those monsters had insatiable appetites for any sort of opening they could get into. And then they would fester there whilst they fed off you.

Mr Moss was different. He was mature, and he would come and sweep her right off her feet. And off they would go, right along Monmouth Street, one of the spokes of that wheel, straight down to Victoria Station; and then from there all the way down to Provence, with her trees pregnant with mimosa.

She did not bother to knock, but opened Edith's door.

Edith was eating a kipper, as if she was knitting. The room reeked.

'You patriotic thing. Because you worked for the Ministry of Agriculture and Fisheries, it doesn't mean that you have to eat North Sea kippers.'

'Oh, Gloria! You haven't asked me why I'm still here.'

'Why? Are you going somewhere?'

'You know I'm going. You know I'm going to Prissy in Carshalton. You haven't asked me why I'm still here.'

Gloria sighed. 'All right, why are you still here? Is it the way I attacked those pseudies last night?'

'Yes, it is because of the way you behaved. But it wasn't last night, it was the night before last.'

'Don't make me laugh.' She laughed. 'You're all liars, all rotting filthy liars. What happened to yesterday? What?'

'What indeed? You tell me. Yesterday you were absolutely incoherent. I nearly dialled 999. Anyway it's all arranged, I'm going tomorrow or at the very latest, the day after. I shall be glad to go.'

'Let's go out and have a lovely cup of coffee.'

'Oh please do be consistent.'

'And even if I was inconsistent, why not? The history of mankind's been pretty consistent and look where we are today. Come on, we mustn't argue, we've known each other far too long.' She hated to speak with such sickening sentimentality. Of course, she had known Edith a few years longer than she had known most people, one could not mercilessly reject just everyone; some people needed a few words of kindness. Besides, you could not pick and choose all the time, so one had to be thankful for small mercies. But it really was a reciprocal thing. Gloria hated the thought of going into a café alone, and she was prepared to allow Edith to accompany her, and participate in her beautiful mood which was now as light as the fluffy sky, and nothing in the world, not even Edith, would make her feel depressed.

'Put away your kipper and come with me. I'm terribly sorry.'

'My umbrella is in smithereens. I shall have to throw it away.' She removed a little bone from her teeth and held it to the light.

'I'm so sick of these new religions; these crooked little religions. Let's get back to a real crooked religion, like Christianity, if we must. Or horrible vegetarianism, or elephant worship. Incidentally, how is Black Midas?'

'Haven't seen him for donkeys years. Please leave me, Gloria, I was enjoying my kipper until you appeared. Now you've spoiled everything.'

'I'm warning you, Edith, I'm heartily sick of you. I'm going out now before you spoil the entire day for me. I shall reimburse you for the umbrella I ruined last night.'

'It wasn't last night.'

'Ruined with every justification, I might add. Go whenever you like. Go as soon as possible, but before you go, open the door to no one, except one rather distinguished-looking gentleman answering to the name of Mr Moss.'

She had practically left the room when something else occurred to her. 'Where's my rent? Where's all my back rent?'

Edith did not look up, but kept her eyes upon the bony carcase as she pointed with a fish knife to the mantelpiece. How strange to have a fish knife in this day and age. Fish knives belonged to the pre-frozen-food era.

Gloria counted the money. 'It's right. But only just, I must have been mad because I never charged you enough. I took pity on you.'

Edith coughed and Gloria slammed the door and went all the way down towards the street, scooping up her beautiful fluffy angora poncho, and throwing it upon herself. She was going back into her real world; the world of people, of real people. The world of Black Midas. And Edith would be left alone for the rest of her days, with her pension from the Ministry of Agriculture and Fisheries, her fish knife and fork, and her little kipper bones held up to the light, to see what trivial little death she had just escaped from.

Poor Edith. She was born Poor Edith and her life had been Poor Edith, and she would die Poor Edith. And that should be her epitaph. 'POOR EDITH.' That would be the inscription on her slab.

Gloria decided not to go straight to find Black Midas, and as she left the house she could see the sad face of Adrian staring out of the perspiring windows of the Come As You Are.

She would go in there for a coffee because everyone needed stepping-stones; oases in the wilderness.

And after that there would be the blissful stimulating company of Black Midas.

8

'Cab!' she called, and it immediately came towards her, and stopped. 'Take me to Powis Square, North Kensington.'

Gloria was glad he was the older sort of cabbie and therefore of the old school; the sort of man who knew his place, and didn't want to engage you in conversation about the soaring price of practically everything and the plummeting morals of teenagers. He didn't even blink his eye to consult a map inside his head, for being of the older school, he was programmed to go straight towards his destination, and by the quickest possible route.

She sank down into the leather to enjoy the security of the vehicle. Cabs were really an extension of one's own home; they carried you through dark landscapes in safety and comfort. She could not have survived without taxi-cabs; the smell and the warmth of them was most reassuring.

And it occurred to her that her reality had almost returned. Her decision to leave the hospital, against the advice of that stupid little gnome, who had somehow managed to get himself qualified as a doctor, had been proved correct. She wished he could see her now; the way she was coping with her life. She had told him many times, she had told so many people so many times, that all she really needed was to just step out of the rat race for a few weeks, and with the minimum of treatment and a few mild sedatives she would soon be raring to go.

It would be bliss to see Black Midas again; to see that old rogue in his den would be a balm for her soul, but because she did not want to become too excited, she popped one of those magic pills into her mouth.

And consequently, there was no sensation of falling through the dark night, the cab was going along the streets horizontally. She was not in a lift hurtling down through empty space into endlessness. Her reflection was superimposed upon the flying-away streets, and her face was real enough because she could see it reflected in the window. And within minutes she would come face to face with Black Midas again. And she could face that.

'Would you please stop chanting the Vedas over my ravioli.' The voice of Black Midas boomed across the past, reprimanding his primary acolyte, Parsival.

Some people you could dredge up quite profitably from the past, they would not destroy you, even though you could not trust them an inch. Just a few people were like this and she was speeding through darkness towards one of them. Black Midas was so crooked that they would probably screw him straight down into the earth when he died. But she had always been able to afford the price of their friendship, it had not rocketed.

London was a cut-out of a city, a deserted lot of a defunct film company. All the buildings were merely pressed out from the cardboard background of the earth. Structures and façades propped forward and without anything behind.

Gloria was delighted as she floated through Paddington, delighted that the voice of Midas had come to her from the past. The past was beautiful and profit-

67

No, nothing had changed, and nothing would change. You could rely upon Black Midas even more than the pips of Greenwich.

'EVERYTHING EXISTS' was painted in gold lettering across the basement wall.

'Midas is in hospital,' he said.

'Oh don't tell me—what for?'

'I fear he's moving on, Gloria.'

'Moving on? Parsival, speak in Wimbledoom. What's he suffering from?'

'He's suffering from life, Gloria.'

'Oh dear, that's a terrible disease.'

'Yes, you never get over it, you're certain to die of it in the end.'

She was absolutely certain that he was absolutely not telling the truth. Parsival loved his mysterious little games, and despite his ferret face was a very loyal acolyte and would have been in tears if Midas were dying. Consequently, she felt very much relieved and her heart pounded at a far more natural pace.

She sat on the floor. 'Didn't you used to have a few more bats hanging on the walls?'

He seemed to go all vacant and then he replied. 'The North Kensington Service is about to begin.'

'You mean the morning service.'

'No, the mourning service; for the death of the sun.' He pulled back a curtain but it made no difference. 'Baby, it's cold outside; and dark.'

'Parsival, it's dark inside, switch on the light, I can't bear this latest fad for interior twilight.'

'We'll switch on the sun as soon as the ladies arrive. It burns a hell of a lot of electricity.'

She suddenly wondered how old he was. There were some people who had no age.

There was a pentagram painted on the floor, and branches and leaves from yester years hanging from the walls. And a poster urging one to travel by British Rail. And a stuffed toucan, and a stuffed orang-utan; and she was sure it was either one or the other that ponged to high heaven. And although both their faces were in good repair, the posterior of the monkey and the belly of the bird had burst open. Not all the Edwardian taxidermists were in the same class, obviously.

'Hello, Gloria my love. How are you, love? Have a cup of tea.' The voice was familiar and so were the fingers as they handed her the steaming teacup and then proceeded to stroke her neck. And the face was familiar.

'Bruce! How are you? How are the teacups?'

'Drink your tea and I'll tell you,' the Astrologer said.

'It's lovely to be amongst your own.' They all joined her on the floor. Nothing had changed.

And she did not mind the youngish man with the shifty eyes and the pockmarked face who came in and sat with them.

'You know Stephanos, don't you?'

She nodded. 'I couldn't fail to forget such an unforgettable face. Who are you?'

'Oh gawd, 'ere she goes agin,' he replied in his Camden Town cockney; flashing his own perfectly white and even teeth.

'Of course, you are coming back to me now. You're the housebreaker. How's business?'

'Mustn't grumble, making a few bob.'

'Don't you ever dare break into Gloria's house, or you'll have to answer to me,' Bruce said, his dry eyes tossing a suggestive caber at his colleague.

'Weren't you inside? For life or something?' Stephanos used to be very pretty a few months before. She used to fall headlong for pretty boys like that, before she grew up. 'I remember your picture in the papers.'

'Yes, he broke a man instead of a house,' Parsival said. 'Don't you wish he'd broken you, Bruce, and not some American tourists?'

'No such luck,' Bruce piped. 'He's wicked. I don't know which way to turn as far as he's concerned.'

'Do you need your windows cleaned, or something?' Stephanos put his arm around her. His breath smelled of garlic sausage. She tried not to shrug away. He stared into her a moment, and she wondered if he really did desperately want to make love to her. After all, she wasn't as desirable as she used to be. On the other hand, she could well imagine a man being obsessed by the unchanging physical beauty she possessed.

She stood up and dismissed him from her mind. She wouldn't let him anywhere near her, not if and when they were alone. But he was beautiful, at a distance, so she walked across the room to stare back at him.

'Fag anyone?' She took out a packet and they all took. 'They're Turkish.'

'Sure they're not grass?'

'I'm no dope fiend. If it's not inside you, darling, it won't come out, whatever you use.' The Turkish cloud joined the Agarbatti and hung above their heads. 'When's Midas coming?'

'I told you, he's not coming. He's going. Going where we're all going.'

'Be sensible, what are we all doing here then without Midas?'

'Carrying on the good work, of course.' Bruce was getting into the golden gown that Parsival had just handed to him.

'It's pay night tonight. We're having a wee drop ot equinox first and the water of life later.'

'You see, Gloria, we mustn't let the business go down the drain. Black Midas would only have it this way. We are expanding and perpetuating our long-term interest in the Solar collateral,' said Parsival.

'So we mustn't sit abaht, lady and gentlemen, the daughters of the sun should start arriving sharpish.' Stephanos looked quite fetching in his golden gown, even if his face did seem a trifle fatty. And Parsival switched on the sun; the great neon sun that covered the whole of one wall. It revolved and it didn't matter that two of the tubes hissed and didn't come on completely; their flickering added a certain air of expectancy. There was no mistaking that this was the sun altar; and all the men stood before it, busy painting their faces with golden patterns.

'Read my teacup please.' She held it forward towards Bruce.

'What are you going to be, Gloria? One of the daughters of the sun, or one of us in the hierarchy? You could be our Mother of the Golden Planets.' Poor Parsival tried so hard to cultivate a Charterhouse twang in his voice.

He held out a golden sackcloth robe, so she slipped into it, and then she sprayed herself with tincture of the universe. 'Please read my cup, Bruce, please tell me what lies in store for me.'

'Yes—this is very inter—' A gong broke his deliberation. 'They'll be descending any minute now,' he said hurriedly, pushing the teacup back into her hand. He moved to a corner where he stood looking at himself far away in thought. She hoped he had not seen anything too terrible in her cup and that the gong had not given him the opportunity to hide from her a horrifying and inevitable tragedy. And now she was angry with herself but not with him. It had been most stupid to want to read the future, the future had to be avoided like the plague. If you ignored it and refused to recognize it, it could not touch you. From now on she would treat the future with the contempt it deserved. That was the only way to deal with it.

And she glowed again like all the sun-ray lamps that Parsival was switching on. She felt warm and strong and so delighted to be amongst such beautiful and interesting dredged-up survivors from that beautiful world of the past. The one thing that could never die; the one thing that was totally reliable.

'You see, Gloria, now that his soul is being swallowed up by the sun, and he's going all yellow, Midas has officially signed over the religion to me.' Parsival switched on the golden ceiling, joined hands with his fellow priests and they all circled around her. 'You put your right foot in, you put your right foot out, you put your right foot in and you shake it all about—'

They were fooling in a worldly, secular fashion, before the serious business began. And they stopped, put their hands high to the heavens and as they brought them down they bowed, right down to the floor. 'Oh hokey cokey cokey, oh hokey cokey cokey—'

She joined in with them and got carried away, far beyond her surface laughter.

9

There was still time to escape, but she was held by her fascination. The antique birds who had descended upon North Kensington were twittering in another room, and Parsival stood rubbing his black paws, so obviously pleased with the turn-out.

The chief acolyte of Black Midas had come into his own, and seemed to enjoy standing in for his master, who would surely be appearing any moment now. And Bruce and Stephanos also seemed to be delighted with their less exalted positions. How they enjoyed suffering from acolytis; that disease of wanting to be close to the source of power, any power; that need to touch the aura of the High Priest.

'But where is he? When is Black Midas coming?'

'I told you, he is never coming. He's a gonner. He's already signed the religion over to me. Excuse me—' Parsival went to a statue that she had not noticed before; it was a huge peeling, golden effigy.

'Who's he when he's awake?'

Parsival turned to shush her. 'Horus!' he said, putting his fingertips to his lips.

She did not personally have anything against Parsival, and she did not exactly hate him; but he was still a loathsome toad. Nevertheless, he was not a stodge person, you had to notice someone so ugly. Ugly people did not grow on trees. And even though the thought of him would be enough to nauseate any normal person, she personally could bear him. He was most loyal to the religion, and loyalty was a very rare commodity nowadays. For however crooked his heart, the look of piety upon his face seemed real enough. And even if the religion was phoney, it probably made some old dears happy; and if you thought you were happy, you were happy.

A gong shattered her criss-crossing deliberations.

'Enter, oh children of Osiris. Come away from Seth, oh ye golden daughters of Isis.'

The golden daughters entered and were all at least sixty years upwards. They came out of the adjoining room and did not bring Seth with them, whoever he was. Gloria was glad of this because she did not have a furious desire to be introduced to Seth at that moment.

She could not make the door, not at that precise moment. Besides, the twenty odd ladies were slowly taking their places in a semi-circle. Consequently, Gloria decided she would sit it out, so she slumped back into the chair that Bruce had just blown up for her with a bicycle pump. But now she kept her eyes on Parsival. He was turned away from the ladies, and he was fussing around the glass-fibre irises which were emitting a high-pitched gurgling sound.

Parsival gave her a sense of security. In a rapidly changing world, he had not changed. A thousand incarnations could not change Parsival, and it made a change to be able to rely upon something. The cataclysm would come and go, and Parsival would still be there, standing upon the top of a pile of devastation, trying to figure out ways of disposing of scrap metal, bricks and glass splinters.

'May you all bathe within the love of Nut and Keb. Take up your goggles.'

'Oh Osiris! Oh Ra! Hear us, Horus!' They all put on their goggles and they threw their hands up, straight to the ceiling and then they all bowed down to the floor. She had to admit that such application certainly improved the appearance of quite a few of them.

'Oh Priests of Ra, gather round. Give golden goggles to the new novices.'

Stephanos and Bruce did the necessary, handing out goggles to the few nervous and obviously new ladies.

She liked the tone of Parsival's adopted voice. It reminded her of those smug little men who gave religious chats on the B.B.C. every morning; those who made you loathe them so much. Yet that confident holier-than-thou tone made you feel good because it was always good to start the day with a curse and a giggle.

'Feeling all right Gloria?' Bruce whispered out of the side of his mouth, and touched her on the shoulder.

'Tell me, what did my tea leaves say?'

'They said that you're going to live long and die happy.'

'How long is long?'

'How long do you like long to be?' He moved away but she was glad that Stephanos stood quite close, she rather liked his smell of garlic and clove; and his sweet sweat.

'Oh ye Priests of Ra, gather round,' Parsival repeated, hissing it out with tremendous authority, so much so, it caused Gloria for the first time to fear him. And the sudden revelation of his authority knocked Midas off the pedestal in her mind. She tried not to panic when she found she could not recapture his face. Perhaps he was going to die.

She tried and tried, but the face of Black Midas would not come back to her.

Stephanos was not there. He was officiating. She had wanted to hold his wrist so much, but she clutched only the air. He had obviously girded his golden gown and had gathered round. But at least she was pleased that he was taking his role of priest of Ra rather seriously. The poor dears of North Kensington needed to get something for their money.

'I welcome the new faces amongst you. In the name of Ubasti and in the name of Hathor I bid you enter the halls of light. The cat and the cow watch over you now that you have come out of Seth. Oh Ra!'

'Oh Ra!' said all the bowing goggled ladies who had to bathe in the sun supplied by the West London Electricity Board. Just the few newcomers were slightly out of synchronization when it came to supplication, and they looked apprehensively to the others for guidance. 'Oh Ra! Oh Ra! Oh Ra!'

'Hoo-rah,' said Stephanos. Then he put his hand over his mouth to swallow his stupidity.

And they all sat cross-legged on the floor while Parsival intoned. 'Oh sky goddess Nut and husband Keb, the earth, out of whom plants and trees grow, out of whom Notting Hill Gate rears its ugly head, out of all this, we look for a sign of fecundity—'

'Oh hear us, Nut and Keb! Oh hear us, Osiris!' They all droned perfectly.

Midas came back to her. The head of Midas, with his flowing grey hair superimposed upon the ferret face of Parsival. And she knew he could not have that terrible disease; it was very cruel of Parsival to joke about a thing like that. People simply did not joke about cancer. She hated even thinking the word.

Another tablet could not possibly do her harm, so she took it. It wasn't very comfortable sitting in one corner of a room that tilted towards you at an incredible angle. She simply had to right the balance before they fell upon her; all those old ladies of North Kensington, and all the furniture. All those old ladies with their eagle and lion heads and their cat faces. And all the furniture that, before her very eyes, had become giant praying mantises.

But soon the tablet would dissolve, and all the murderous elements in the room would go back to being what they were. Human beings and furniture would know their places once more.

'Oh brother Ammon and brother Pteh, and oh sister Nephthys, switch on Ra the sun God, switch on I say.'

Bruce and Stephanos moved around as if in a trance. They switched off some lights and switched on some more, 'Click! Click! Click!'

Parsival threw her some goggles, and she put them on quickly, as the lights changed in the room. And he pointed like a pre-Hebrew deity at the one switch in her corner of the room.

'Nephthys obeys, oh master.' She got up very slowly.

'So be it, Isis.'

'Who am I? Nephthys or Isis?' She really wanted to know, but fortunately no one had heard her little outburst. All the ladies with their blue-tinted hair seemed to be swaying like hypnotized serpents, so she did what she was told and switched on her own corner. It was all very much of an effort in the throbbing red interior.

And it was just as well that her tears were falling inward as she envied all the others in the room. If only she could have belonged to one side or the other. The victors or the victims. Though which was which, she couldn't really say. If only she could have been a grey lady of Notting Hill Gate; if only she could have got carried away like them.

'Bathe in the sun. Bathe in the rays of the golden sun and live forever. Meet all your dead departed again, in the bright burning halls of the immortal sun. Oh Ra!'

'Oh Ra!' she said. 'Oh Ra!' But she was glad she did not amen too loudly, because it was quite possible that Parsival would have asked her for some money. On the other hand, she was officiating, so possibly one would cancel out the other. 'Oh Ra!' she said more loudly. 'Ra! Ra! Ra! Ra! Ra!' How she longed for the real sun.

'Oh sky bearer! Oh Thinis! Oh Onouris—'

'Oh God,' she wanted it to be over.

But now they all joined Parsival. It was rather like a communal rendering of the Lord's Prayer.

'Oh god of Thinis, you who hold heaven and earth apart, keep Seth away from us. We of the divine cult. Send us Hathor so that we may be depicted as a cow in her image; so that we may be accepted into the house of Horus forever and ever. KEEP SETH AWAY! COME NOT SETH TODAY. OH RA! OH RA! OH RA!'

'You will never die. You will be reunited with your dead husbands and sons and daughters. Let the life-giving rays of Ra enter you. Open your hearts, oh ye daughters. Bare your breasts.'

Gloria wondered if that was strictly necessary, but noticed, to her intense relief, Parisval indicating that she need not comply. Not that she would have done, anyway.

The room was not tilting so crazily now, and the

human faces were returning, and the door leading to the street was not quite so uphill. So, despite the tittering ladies revealing their ugly tits, she felt very much better. 'Where there's life there's hope. So the stupid saying goes,' she muttered. She did not find it within herself to watch the ladies exposing themselves, so she looked at Parsival, and at Bruce and at Stephanos, but they apparently were not denying themselves the pleasure of feasting their eyes upon the raw flesh. Instead, they ogled through their goggles at the semi-circle of standing corpses.

'Oh Isis, oh wives of Osiris, now the sun god has entered you, and Seth has been defeated. Go now!'

Somewhere the triumphal march from *Aïda* was playing, and all the ladies marched around triumphantly to the clashing of cymbals; to the crashing trumpet blast. 'May the life-giving rays of immortal Ra enter you and stay with you.'

Each woman in turn went towards Parsival the High Priest and his two associates, and each had both her nipples daubed with golden paint.

'Return now to the reality of earth. Come back Thursday. Same time, same place. Ra!'

Parsival raised his arms and his assistants switched off the infra or the ultra, and everything was peaceful and quiet as the ladies put on their overcoats, for Ra would not be so apparent in the sky above Notting Hill Gate.

'In the name of Ra and of Horus and of Isis, I bless you. I give you immortality. May you live forever.'

'God help us, I hope not,' Gloria muttered.

'You have come into the golden halls of Ra, you have received the gift of golden light and now you shall, in return, give unto us your trifling items of worldly

81

gold, before ye depart into the world of Seth. Give wrist watches, brooches, or mere money, that Ra shall know, shall recognize and replenish, and give in return gold for gold, perpetuating perpetually.'

As they went out it appeared that most of them were giving mere money. But each face seemed happier than it did when it entered, so who was she to complain? Then all the smiling faces were gone, suddenly. Just like that. That was always the remarkable thing about a room full of people, you only had to turn your head, or have a short conversation, to find that when you looked back, they were all gone.

Parsival held on to the plate that now was full of money, hand fingering the coins and separating them from the pound notes.

'We did very well this evening. Thank you, Gloria. Want a job? I was thinking of sending around to the Employment Exchange for an out-of-work actress. We'll take you on full time as Nephthys.'

'No, I'm afraid it's Isis or nothing.' They were all changing back now.

'All right then, let's go and have some ices.'

But she did not laugh, nor like him any better for his little joke, and she felt uneasy.

'KALI SHIVA, KALI SHIVA, SHIVA SHIVA, KALI KALI...' But it did not work, her sound petered out and Parsival switched out the last of the lights and she was glad to leave the room that stank of incense and scared old ladies; and relieved to follow Parsival upstairs into the cold street.

'I am just going to see Midas before he slips away. Coming, Gloria?'

'Heh, you haven't given us our share yet.' She looked at Bruce and Stephanos as they went towards their new master. And even though they all continued to smile, there was no mistaking the thick air of menace that hung over all their heads. So she moved slightly away from them.

But there was no need for alarm, for Parsival proceeded to give them both their share.

'Goodbye, boys,' she called, but they barely noticed her. They just slipped away, both wearing upholstered smiles, both going in opposite directions. She waved her hands at no one and then she returned to Parsival who stood before her.

'Well, is the religion safe in my hands?' He was clutching some pound notes in his fists. 'To Black Midas then. The taxi's on me.'

'No, take me home.'

'Right you are, we go the same way. Midas is at Charing Cross Hospital. We'll kill two birds with one stone.'

She walked with him, as all the ghosts quickly clustered round all the doors of all the streets.

'How about a partnership? We could do great things together.' His eyeballs rolled, and she felt a great need to get back to Covent Garden.

'I'm sorry, I'm fully employed staying alive.'

She had to get away from there, because it was always the same; that same terrible smell of death, of suicide. It always persisted around Notting Hill Gate. So she was somewhat relieved to see a taxi-cab. She hailed and it sailed towards them. But before it actually stopped, Parsival jerked her into a doorway.

'Let's forget Midas for the moment. Quick! In here, come on. It's no good; you can't resist it.'

He was right. He knew he was. Sometimes it was impossible to fight the inevitable, sometimes you simply had to behave like other human beings and let natural functions take over completely. Besides, she now knew that she needed it very badly.

'Food! Why do I always forget to eat?'

He laughed, and so did she as she followed him into the pie shop. It may have been a far cry from Ra and Isis, but she was very partial to hot jellied eels and mashed potatoes.

10

She had agreed to go with Parsival and visit Black Midas, but now she regretted it. She hadn't wanted to go in the first place, but the nasty little squirt who still walked beside her had somehow managed to make her change her mind.

But now she decided to change it right back.

'I'm going home. I'll visit Midas another time.'

'There may not be another time,' he snorted.

'Anyway, my head is splitting and I don't feel up to it.' She was pleased that home was just around the corner. Notting Hill always gave her the willies.

She crossed Cambridge Circus but still she could not shake him off. 'Look Parsleyballs, please leave me alone.' But when she turned the corner she was glad of company, for she noticed a cluster of little men standing against the hoardings near the door of her home.

The fishmonger nodded as she got near, and Gloria wondered how he could possibly earn a living selling wet fish in an area that was dying the death. But his blown-up hands were still raw and red; so obviously business had not slackened off. Even now he was filleting a cod, turning a recognizable creature into oblong edible portions.

The men near her home did not really worry her. No power on earth could remove her from Neal Street;

not even Holborn Borough Council. She was not afraid of them; whoever they were.

Gloria wasn't drunk enough, it was no use being left high and dry, halfway upon the warm dark sea. And then she realized that she had stopped walking, and she and Parsival were standing by the fishmonger's stall.

'It's nice to see you again, Miss Gaye. Will you be wanting anything Friday?'

'This Friday and every Friday. Incidentally, if a rather distinguished-looking man, with silver hair, comes asking for me, tell him I have not moved out, nor am I likely to.' She pointed to the group of little men. 'Who are they?'

'Surveyors, I think.'

'Surveyors of death.'

The fishmonger laughed, pulled out a tail from a box of ice, and started humming to himself. And she sailed away towards her familiar territory.

'Why do you persist in following me?' She still felt nothing but contempt for this Parsival. He may have been adequate when it came to running a religion, but he was no match for the master. Black Midas had style and grace. 'Please stop following me.'

'I thought you might change your mind and come to Midas. He could go any moment.'

'Yes I must see Midas. But in my own time. I am more concerned about other things.'

She turned around and walked away from the house. When three men stood together in a group, they were up to no good.

She recrossed the Circus, and as usual, it was full of clowns. Every tightrope walker, every deathly trapeze artiste was falling upon his face, and a great wave of black gnawing emptiness clutched at her from within

86

her stomach; the bony fist of death was tearing out her entrails.

Parsival continued to trail along beside her, so she decided to make him pay for the honour.

'Very well, you may buy me a drink.' She could see the oasis York Minster ahead. There would be a gathering of people quenching their thirst there; ridding themselves of the loneliness of the desert of existence.

'With pleasure.' Parsival pushed the door open for her.

She liked the mass of familiar faces; it was reassuring.

'Yes, one needs sustenance to face the death of Midas. Brandy?'

He elbowed his way to the counter and she followed. 'Yes please, a double.' Parsival may not have been born pretty, but he was an excellent dogsbody.

'Cheers.' The beautiful forest fire raged through her. Every part of her was burning down, and so wonderfully. 'Imagine Black Midas seeping back into the universe via Charing Cross Hospital.' She looked around, everyone was looking lovely today.

'Still, his religion's in safe hands. And sod the universe. What's the universe ever done for me? I need another drink.' She handed him the empty glass. He fell over himself to obey.

'Hello, Gloria. How are you, love?'

'I'm wonderful, darling, how are you?'

'I'm marvellous, darling, how are you?'

She looked around at the face and wasn't at all happy that Parsival had been swallowed up near the counter. But his hand did come through with her glass replenished, so she gladly turned to the face that was kissing her other hand. Then she realized it was the face of that awful man. 'Aren't you that journalist man ... James?'

'I am, darling, and I love you dearly; and do forgive me. And let me buy you a drink.'

Suddenly she warmed to him; people were not as bad as you knew they were. Suddenly all was forgiven, and you could relax into the familiarity, peace and security of anyone, as long as it was a face you had seen before and it did not fall upon you with icy cold fangs that ripped into your flesh, sucked out your blood, and tore you to pieces.

She realized she was clutching him. 'Thank you, poppet. I'll have a double brandy please.'

He was much fatter than Parsival, who seemed to have disappeared for the moment. This one brought back the drink every time, and brought his face with it. And she liked his face more and more. He stayed with her, it was good to have a companion, above the earth or beneath it. 'Darling, I'm absolutely pissed and I'm glad. And to think I hated you this morning.'

'Why this morning?'

'You know, when you came to my door for a story. Because you can be very stupid, and very boring sometimes.'

'But I didn't come this morning. It must have been three or four days ago. But don't let's talk about it.' Jimmy was so lovely and it just proved that you could be so wrong about people. And somehow, she didn't mind that he had lost track of time. Everyone seemed to be losing track of time, but then perhaps this was all to the good. After all, there was no reason why there should be continuity. Continuity had not done the world any favours. Days following each other, in sequence, had not exactly made the earth a safe place to live upon. She could put up with the loss of continuity as long as the golden liquid from the fruit of the earth could pour down her throat, glow before her eyes, and sail her gently beyond all the dark shores of flesh and bricks.

She kissed Jimmy on the forehead, and did not know how much time had passed in the world. 'The trouble is, people don't rip you to pieces any longer.'

One could excuse an assassination; a murder of extreme passion with daggers and blood. One could certainly excuse cannibalism. The trouble was that nobody would go that far. Everyone just wanted a very thin slice of everyone. They whittled away slice by slice, and then passed you on to the next slicing machine.

'Yes darling, just sign here please.' Jimmy smiled, looking so pink and chubby.

She looked around for Parsival, because that was the face that she needed. The face to take her to the place where she would face Midas. And Parsival was there, looming up beyond the wall of familiar faces, but he was just out of focus. She wondered how long she had been there, and how long she had talked to this lovely man, Jimmy. She loved people who allowed her to sail on through all the oceans of her life, talking about all her days; the storms, the calms, the hates, the loves. How she loved to be able to talk to a listener. Listeners were so rare these days. And Jimmy was a gem; the way he just smiled as she trotted out all the events that led up to now. She could tell him anything. He didn't even mind her revelations about Belton, where she had gone to relieve the pressure of that awful birth of the book; that murder by indifference, when she had seen her own afterbirth thrown away by a total lack of understanding, by those literary critics who once had been her gods. None of them believed just how fabulous, full and passionate her past had been; and here at last was a real human being willing to listen, proving perhaps that there was still some decency and kindness left in the world.

'Please sign here. Here.'

'It just shows how wrong you can be about people. I hated you. I thought you were a toad.'

She took the drink in one hand, and the silver pen in the other, and she poured down one and was about to pour out the other. 'You do well to get my autograph, while you can get it for free.' She scrawled her full name right across the page to show that she was alive and would live forever. And she kissed him on the mouth. 'My autograph, Jimmy darling.'

'Yes, your autograph. Thank you very much. And one for the road?' His eyes were running away from her, so she supposed it was only right that he should follow.

'Please take care of my autograph. It's the only one I've got.' She drained down the drink, right down her diagonal self. And she stood up, emerging upon the surface of bloated faces, waving waves.

Time does not take the flesh away immediately. It adds before it subtracts; it deals in sponges. Time was a make-up artist, sponges for the inside of the cheeks and spray for the hair. And the gradual drifting away from the lighted area, into the silent alleyways of earth.

And he was gone, James the beautiful sincere journalist. And Parsival was there to lead her to Black Midas who would be departing from the neon dockland of Charing Cross. It was time to go.

'Time, gentlemen, please!' The voice boomed several times over, agreeing with her. People were reluctant to go, but sometimes feet knew better; they knew you had no real choice.

11

Gloria was glad that Midas could wait just a little longer for her visit; after all, he would be dead for a long time.

'Isn't it funny, one never bumps into Dylan Thomas these days.'

'But, Gloria, Dylan's dead.'

'What's that got to do with it?'

And at that precise moment she thought she could actually see dear Dylan going up the alleyway, past the side door of her own butchers. She wondered what the poet could possibly be up to along the Seven Dials, at that time of day? Or night? So she left Farcical Balls and trundled towards the smell of lard and congealed blood.

'Dylan, what are you doing sitting in that doorway dressed as a tramp?'

'Hello, Gloria, give us a cigarette?'

She lit one, and gave it to him. The whole corner glowed as he sucked in the smoke.

'Where have you been, Dylan? I've missed you.'

'I've been dead actually.'

'Really? Oh, what's it like?'

'Very nice, thank you very much. Gloria, loan us two hundred and fifty quid, there's a love.'

'I don't think I have that amount at the moment.'

'Gloria, what are you doing along there? Who are you talking to?'

'Oh, no one. Just talking to Dylan Thomas.' But when she turned back, poor Dylan was gone.

'Bye bye Dylan love. Dylan; My mackerel-headed, tawny-thighed, trumpet-tongued, emery-paper-throated minstrel boy. Sorry about the cash. See you soon! See you soon!'

She blew some kisses into the twilight sky. They were soon swallowed up by the thankful ravenous fog.

'In yonder green valley where streamlets meander,' Gloria sang, and then she went straight into, 'The minstrel boy to the war is gone, in the ranks of death you'll find him,' but realizing it was Irish and not Welsh, she dropped it and wept dryly and silently, and walked out of the passage back to where Parsival was waiting for her. 'We'll be late for Midas.'

'Let's go home first and have a party, to celebrate.'

'To celebrate what?'

But she was already ahead of him, and opening her door. 'Come to a party. Come to a party everyone! Come to a party! Dylan, where are you? You're invited.' But no voices replied. 'Tutankhamen, where are you?'

But there were no miaows, no voices of people living, or dead. 'Karen, my lovely little Karen, come back, come back.' There was the shivering and creaking of the wind, trying to break through the wooden hoardings.

'Gloria, why are you crying?'

'Shut up, Parsival, before I shut you up.' Who was he to want to know? 'It's just water flowing out of my eyes. I'm not crying.'

Who could know her grief? Who wanted to know the grief of a grandmother who only wanted to forget a grand-daughter, however beautiful; living or dead? 'Oh Karen.' No one, but no one had been more beautiful than the child; and no one had died so tragically.

Gloria rubbed away her tears. There was no Karen. There was no death of Karen. And she was no grandmother. How absurd! She was Gloria Gaye!

Edith was sitting in her room in her faded, torn, spermless kimono.

'Edith, what are you doing in my room?'

'I just want to see you, to chat, to say goodbye before I go.'

'No, don't go, we're having a party. Parsival, put on some lovely music, and pour us all a drink. Edith, why aren't you happy? You're only dead forever. Were there any phone calls?'

'No. No phone calls.'

'Why not?' She went straight to the telephone and dialled the hospital. It was engaged. 'It's been engaged a long time. It's not respectable to be engaged for so long, without the prospect of marriage. Did anyone come?'

Looking out of the window, she was not sure if it was day or night, summer or winter, or if the city was on fire, or not.

'Is it tomorrow yet?' she asked herself.

'It's always tomorrow. If you think today's yesterday.'

How could they understand what she meant? How could they know that she had been a very sensitive child and used to look at the atlas of the world each morning?

'It's like when you breathe in, you inhale the spores of death. We'll gather lilacs in the spring again,' she sang just one line. Ivor Novello often made her feel too emotional.

'Come on cheesy toes, or Fartiballs, or whatever your name is, you will have to do.'

She danced with him. 'Edith, drink some green

93

Chartreuse, it goes with your complexion. Perhaps I'll tinkle dear Noël or Terence, or that delightful man Sir Henry Moore.'

She dialled decisively. 'Oh, hello dear, could you possibly connect me with Transatlantic Enquiries. Thank you.' She smiled and only had to wait a few moments. 'Oh hell, I wish to talk to Mr Tennessee Williams and I wondered if you knew where he might be—? Now listen my dear, how could I possibly know? It's your job to know where someone is. Now listen, honey. No, no, just listen—' The young man may have had a cultured voice, but that did not necessarily include him amongst the blessed of the earth. 'Look, he could be anywhere. In New Orleans, Cannes, or even possibly he's eating at the Savoy Grill. Look, I'm not putting up with any more of your lip, I'd like to talk to your supervisor.'

Parsival passed round the box of Turkish Delight. He had been fingering the top layer, so she dug down for a clean piece, and settled back as he danced unusually close to the concave Edith. 'Oh! Oh! I shouldn't really, I should be packing.' The lady from the Min of Ag and Fish squeaked and giggled.

'Oh hell, how do you do. This is Miss Gloria Gaye speaking. The Gloria Gaye. And I'm trying to get hold of Mr Tennessee Williams. Yes, Tennessee, as in the Confederation of Southern States.'

The woman or man was polite. And stupid.

'Yes Tennessee Williams, THE Tennessee Williams. The playright who once asked me, THE Gloria Gaye, to play Blanche Dubois in THE original production of *A Streetcar Named Desire*. Oh shut up, you silly stupid cow!' She slammed down the receiver, breathed deeply to calm herself, and then dialled Belton again. This time it rang, and rang. But there was no reply. The man at the switchboard was probably having it off with a melancholy bank clerk behind the rhododendrons. Fancy taking advantage of someone in the throes of a breakdown.

'Someday I'll find you, moonlight behind you,' she glided to the window humming. Down at the door she could see her unmistakable darling boys, Charles and Larry. And it suddenly dawned upon her. They had been the strange men she had seen earlier; either today or yesterday, or the day before. But what did it matter? That was surely the whole point of not having to slog your guts for a living. You were not a prisoner of time; you were not a slave; you could manage very well without the stupid continuity of the everyday world. It was so lovely to be your own boss. That was, of course, if you were not a slave driver.

There was never a sound more welcome than the knocking that reverberated through the stomach of her house.

'It's Charles and Larry, I knew they hadn't left me, I knew.' But Edith and Parsival were dancing the tango. She interrupted them, pulled the bony shoulder of the woman. Edith was asleep. Little pieces of Turkish Delight were still clinging to her top lip.

'A moustache helps,' she said.

Parsival tangoed his partner towards the sofa, and let her fall away from him. Edith went backwards, straight down, rather pleasantly. The thin cool smile was still maintained on the face of the head, that had shrunk to the size of a grapefruit. And all since the day before.

'Science is a very wonderful thing,' Gloria said. 'Black-balls, help yourself to Turkish Delight.'

Edith snored and dreamed of kippers. She was deep

95

in the arms of Murphy, the Irish god of sleep. The Irish were a most compassionate race, even Edith could enter into their heaven.

'I slept last night with a Grenadier Guardsman.' Gloria knew the words were wrong, but she was quite sure that Ivor Novello would not mind. She sailed all the way down the stairs, humming the plaintive melody, until she reached the door. All she had to do was open it. Her darling boys would be on the other side.

12

'Gloria darling, we heard you were back.'

She disentangled herself from the sickening embrace of the two bald-headed men. Gloria could have sworn it had been her boys at the door, but here were two secret agents from Holborn Borough Council trying to force their way into the house.

'Gloria darling, it's us. It's me, Larry.'

She realized that she had come downstairs with a breadknife, yet she had not been cutting bread; and she wondered why they still persisted in their stupid deception.

Both were middle-aged, fat, and obviously up to no good. When strangers came smiling at your door, they never came for your good, they always wanted something from you.

'Get away! Get away!' She heard herself screaming, but she declined to brandish the breadknife above her head. 'What do you want?' Her mind raced upstairs, to that police whistle she had placed in the garlic bowl, in the kitchen. But there was simply no point chasing upstairs after her mind; because even if she managed to blow that whistle, there would be no response from the Metropolitan Police, because, after all, defending yourself from assault was not in the same category of crime as parking on a double yellow line.

'Do you mind?' She tried pushing one of them away

from her, but of course she was no match for even one male torso, no matter how flabby and middle-aged it was.

'Parsival,' she called, though she knew even that was no use. She had seen the way his eyes had caressed that frail fishbone Edith. He was otherwise engaged in the romantic foreplay of necrophilia.

'Who are you? Who sent you? Go back to the Town Hall where you belong.'

'Gloria! You are such a mad thing. It's been aggers not seeing you. It's us, Larry and Charles! Have we changed that much in six months?' The Larry one giggled towards his accomplice. 'She does go on, but then she always did.'

'Parsival, please help me,' she called up the endless stairs.

Now they both laughed and the Charles one pirouetted to where she was, clicked on the electric light and poised himself like a grinning piece of cheesecake beneath the forty watt bulb.

'Oh she's wicked, she's utterly wicked. She's terribly bold and frightfully naf, but we adore her.'

Gloria sat down on the stairs, for of course it was them. But she did not chide herself for not recognizing them, it was they who had changed. And so quickly. Everything was changing quickly, streets were narrowing and closing down, the sky had given up the ghost long ago, and the people were not nice any more. The softness in their faces, and the dream in their eyes had gone. They were all overfed and under par; sub-clinical suburbanites, like these two unfortunate fattening souls who had once been her darling boys.

'Hello Larry. Hello Charles. It hasn't been six months, you fools. What's happened to you?'

'We came to see you specially, and to collect the last

98

of our things that we left behind.'

'We live, as you know, in Dollis Hill. It's deathly dull, but one has to move with the times.'

'It's not as respectable as all that, get you Charlotte. We have quite an up and coming gay coterie in Dollis Hill. It's as camp as old Chloe.'

'We simply loathed leaving you, Gloria, but we had no choice.'

'No, not once that frightful eviction order was served. Doesn't do to get on the wrong side of the law, if you don't know which way to turn.' The laughter bellowing out of both was sick-making.

'There will be no eviction from this house,' she used her steel-like intonation, but then she shrugged off her Mother Courage act. 'But do what you like. Go where you will. I'm going upstairs.'

'May we come up, Gloria?'

'I suppose you have to.'

She was glad they had moved away. It was far better for people who could not face the future, to sink into the shades of N.W.2. 'Up you come then, you silly boys.'

She decided to be slightly hospitable, for even they could feel the obvious gulf between them, and they would not come again, and for that she was truly thankful. It was very hurtful to see the way time ravaged some people, so suddenly. Everyone that you once cared for. Now she knew that she could relinquish everyone. Everyone except Mr Moss. In the end, people were as dispensable as plastic teacups. They could be left behind after the picnic. People were eminently replaceable, all disposable things were replaceable. Still, she liked people. She had not grown to hate those she could live without; indeed, most people in the world were worthwhile, but that was exactly why she could dispense with most of them. You had to draw the line somewhere. And that line was drawn around your own silhouette. For in the end, you could only rely upon yourself, and even so, when the body became punctured, the essential essence of you slipped through the barricade of life and you seeped out, and you were overtaken by battalions of worms.

'Yes, if you like.' She had heard them ask for something and she couldn't very well turn them away, without a by-your-leave.

'Goody, we have nice drinky coffee.'

They followed her upstairs, towards tangoing Parsival, who still thumped around the room with eyeballs rolling. The whites of his eyes was the only white he could show, from his forehead down to his ankles. They entered the open door.

'We brought you a lovely present,' Charles beamed.

She took the plastic flower, quite graciously. 'It's very nice, darling.'

'One should always give plastic flowers. After all, they never die.'

'We thought it was just you.'

'Coffee?' She made the sign of a cup being upturned near her mouth. 'Coffee for my lovelies? Or Dubonnet?'

'Oh, we are having a party, how gay.'

Edith unwound to a standing position, and stared into the hand she held against her face. It was as if she were about to reveal the secret of the universe. They went over, gaggled around her, but she hurled a few icy darts, so it was hardly surprising that they returned to her; to their one and only Gloria Gaye. And she poured out the red wine for them.

'Mustn't stay long. And we mustn't have more than one little drink, at the most. After all, we're not as young as we used to be.'

'No, you are not, are you?'

Someone screamed outside. It could have been human, or on the other hand, it could have been Tutankhamen. She rushed to the window, but it was only a seagull circling high above the hotel, two streets away. 'Disgusting creatures. Pigeons in disguise.'

Larry and Charles were both red in the face by now. The red wine had obviously gone straight to their heads.

'Isn't it way past your bedtime, boys?' For she feared the worst. And then it happened. Larry lay on the floor. and Charles clambered on top of him, and they began their most celebrated act, the one she had seen a thousand times, the one that had thrilled audiences all over Lancashire.

They went through their contortions with smiling faces that did not hide their fear, and she was afraid for them, and afraid for the floorboards. For the fairies were not as fairylike as they once were.

'Come on darlings, Dollis Hill needs you.'

Charles' upside down face yawned. 'We really must keep ourselves polished.'

But Larry was puffing, and purple round the chops.

'Come on sweet baby, we've to to sign on at the Labour tomorrow.' Charles groaned as he stood up.

'Very well, take me back to Dollis Hill and destroy me.'

They creaked to their feet, and they automatically stood together and went straight into a horrible soft-shoe shuffle. 'We don't know know which way to turn, who's on top, or on the ground. But we try to stay with the bold and gay, as we keep turning round.' It was most pathetic.

'I really should be packing now,' Edith lay there showing her crotch, which fortunately was covered with pink knicker. 'In A Persian Market' was playing, and the formation of seagulls vortexed in the still free sky out of the window.

'I really must get on with the packing,' Edith said.

'And we must be going to Midas,' Parsival said.

'Yes, why don't you,' Gloria said.

Larry laughed at her audacity, but his hilarity was soon overtaken by a fit of coughing, and he spluttered his way out of the room.

She left the room with them, revealing how remarkably kind she could be, sometimes.

'You haven't changed one little bit, Gloria.'

'No, she hasn't changed one teeny bit.'

'You two, I'm afraid, have changed quite considerably.'

Parsival went on ahead and opened the door for them. She hadn't wanted to hurt them but now she needed to. It would do them good in the long run. 'Perhaps it's just as well you have given up the business.'

'We haven't really, we're merely resting.'

But Larry was the female of the two, and therefore he was the more honest. 'And we can do with the rest. After all, we are getting a bit long in the tooth for contortions. Poor Charles had terrible backache, and I'm getting terribly stuffy and do need some silly old security in my old age.'

She turned. There was a gaping hole in an advertisement. A funeral parlour once flourished behind that line of smiling dollies. She pressed her face into the opening. 'Tuti! Tuti! Tutankhamen! Puss! Puss! Puss! Puss! Puss!'

Parsival took out a black cigarette with a golden tip, stuck it into an amber cigarette holder and lit it at the sixth attempt, shielding the action with his black paws. And for all that time, no one spoke.

'Oh, it's so lovely being with gay people again.'

The statement fell into a trough of silence that was only broken by a rumble from the lower part of Mr Parsival. 'Excuse me. Caviare doesn't agree with me, that's why I never eat the stuff.' He grinned; she didn't like that at all. His face without any expression was hard enough to bear.

'Well darlings, we're going south, Charing Cross, and you're going north, Dollis Hill.'

'Yes, and we'll all meet up at Mount Pleasant sorting office next Christmas, with a bit of luck.'

She wanted to say so much, but it was not nice to speak disparagingly about the dead. Her lovely boys had died. Her pretty, cheeky contortionists had disappeared off the face of the earth. These creatures were something she hadn't bargained for and consequently she did not need to feel guilty in dismissing them, even though the poor things had been struck by that dread disease, galloping senility, and both at the same time. But perhaps that was only to be expected. They had always been very close, and had done whatever that sort of person did, every night of the year, upon her good mattresses; mattresses that she had replaced every so often because of their horrible necessities. It didn't bear thinking about, but at least it could have been worse. They could have been lesbians and could have had synchronized curse or menopause, on top of everything else. All in all, it just didn't bear thinking about. Yes, it was all to the good, they had gone, her darling boys were dead. And in a moment, these two would go back to Dollis Hill on the Bakerloo Line, forever.

'Puss! Puss! Puss! Puss! Puss!'

But then Gloria realized she would never see Tutankhamen again. She would have to face it. Not that she thought Tuti was dead, or in trouble. No, that was out of the question. The truth was that he had been stolen by an Abyssinian princess who could have been staying at the hotel just across the road.

Yes, she had stayed there for a few days. 'And that's where you are. Abyssinia.'

Gloria wondered why she hadn't thought of that before. But she was very relieved now, and she had nothing against the princess. In fact, she rather loved her. Imagine having the good taste to steal such a superb cat off the streets of London, and imagine having the courage to hide him in that second-class hotel; and to feed him on titbits of lamb and chicken and Dover sole. And then to take all that trouble to smuggle him back to Addis Ababa. Such application, such adoration, warranted only admiration.

It was such a tremendous relief, for Gloria was not kidding herself. There would be trouble tomorrow or the day after. Those eunuchs of the Town Hall would not let her off the hook, and there would be a great fight ahead. The outcome of that fight was in no doubt, but Gloria now knew that she could fight with a much freer and more determined hand knowing that Tutankhamen was safe and well, frolicking amongst the pomegranate groves, and catching jumping fish in the Blue Nile. 'Goodbye Tuti! The Thames flows all the way right down to you, and it contains all my love.'

'Yes,' he said. 'Yes.' The fat, wincing, mincing contortionist, the stupid panting poof was now lifting up the last of his belongings from the street and was ready for the final embrace.

But she decided otherwise, and walked away, followed by Farcical Balls.

'Goodbye boys, see you again some day.'

They were rather stunned, and spluttered fishlike for a moment. 'If you're ever near Dollis Hill, look us up.'

'Hardly,' she said through her teeth, but they did not hear and they waved and waved as she walked away.

She didn't look back but she knew that they were still standing there, and slowly waving, and sadly amused at her most daring, original disappearing act.

'Come Parsival. A sing-song! One day my heart will awake—' She crooned over the empty street, glad that the one who usually shadowed her had given up the ghost; at least for the moment.

And she was even more glad when the stiff but smelly follower of Black Midas chimed in with his crackling falsetto.

'One day the morning will break, sunshine will rise to the skies, and we will fly, to the hereafter.' Gloria knew the words were wrong, but she didn't mind. She continued singing because life was so unbearable, yet it was so lovely to be alive. And at least she wasn't being spied upon and followed at the moment.

And although she looked back, just to be on the safe side, she did not stop singing.

13

'Poor old Midas, everything used to turn to gold for him.'

'Yes, but he lost his touch.' Gloria believed it now, and had resigned herself to seeing him. Certain things could not be avoided.

She was glad she was wearing her vintage Persian lamb. It kept the Whitehall wind from sweeping through her bones.

There was a taxi with its For Hire sign alight, and immediately she put her hand out. It came and stopped, but she shooed it away. Her hand was programmed for taxis. They were her one extravagance in life, apart from all the love and lovers she had so blissfully enjoyed. Tonight she felt like walking, slowly, towards the river.

'It's spitting,' Parsival said. And he was absolutely right, because the sky did start spitting upon them as soon as Trafalgar Square swung into vision at the other end of St Martin's Lane. 'Good!' It would mean that the streets would not be so crowded. And she watched the passers-by hurrying for shelter. Gloria had always been amazed at the way people scuttled like frightened ants, away from the open sky, whenever a drop of water fell. Their prehistoric origins seemed to determine their actions at the slightest hint of natural danger. Yet, what was more dangerous than a man left alone by himself, sheltering in a doorway? Who would use a man more stupidly and more wickedly than man himself?

Or a woman, if it came to that, or those things in between a man and a woman?

'I'm so pleased to be able to wish Midas bon voyage. Why are you sniffing, Parsival?'

'Can't you smell something?'

She tried, but it smelled no differently than usual. It always came out the same. 'I smell the sea, but then I always smell the sea.'

The sea was waiting to pounce and to cover everything. The sea put up with us for a long time, it had sent its murky fingers into every city; dark and slowly it was creeping forward, and now it was ready to assume its original authority, and it would choke the living life out of the land. The sea had been very patient up until now, but it could afford to be magnanimous. One only had to look at the simplest map to see her dominions, and how she waited to reclaim the rest of her planet. It was very comforting to know that we would not have to slither along the mud much longer. One could only breathe a sigh of relief that we had failed our apprenticeship.

He was still sniffing the night.

'What can you smell, Parsival?'

'The end of the world. Can't you?'

'Yes, I believe I can.'

He looked at her in such a strange way. She didn't care for that sort of expression, which was far more concerned with bed than with cataclysm.

'You're a very attractive woman, Gloria, and I've been thinking. Midas is going off to that great scene in the sky, and he's leaving his religion and the whole of festering mankind to myself, Parsival Crouch. Therefore, I shall be a man of considerable substance, so I thought that—'

Certain things needed to be swerved away from. 'Stop thinking, Parsival, and continue sniffing the end of humanity.' She now decided that she would always keep at least three feet away from him. 'So how will the world end?'

He sniffed again, all the way round the sky. 'By fire. I smell burning. I smell the cataclysm. I smell burning flesh and scorched bones.'

She sniffed, and it wasn't quite the same for her. 'There we differ. I smell sea weed and mouldy wood, and mud. The end of the world will be water.'

'This is the manifesto of Parsival Crouch. Take off your clothes before the cataclysm,' he shouted. And she was pleased to notice that no one noticed. 'As long as you don't practise what you preach, Parsival.'

She was not really walking. She was falling down towards the hospital, and he was falling beside her. London was being wiped out and it was a great act of mercy. She hoped it would come before Friday morning, or by Monday at the latest. She giggled as she saw her nasty little men from the Town Hall. They were gouging out each other's eyes, as they tried to swim, up from the sunken chambers of Holborn, out of the twisted flesh of the city. The victorious one rejoiced when he reached the surface, but the victory was pointless and short-lived. For there, above all, he crumbled to dust; sprinkling down as confetti upon the silent, submerged, silver streets.

Gloria sighed. 'Heigh ho, Rome wasn't built in a day.' She had to be a little patient, because the earth had to be walked upon while it was there. The octopus city, that had longings for the sea, was still spreading out and growing while it was dying. Encroaching crystals of black jet were criss-crossing the sky. Plastic erections that were heaps for the living dead, poked the panting sky that hung above her, with its head down. The nailed city. Had it not been a waking nightmare, Gloria could have imagined that a cool enemy, or some rather gay friends, had removed her overnight while she slept, and taken her to Birmingham or some Brasilia of the future; removed her by silent zeppelin.

She wasn't going to the hospital, the hospital was coming towards her. And it was just as well, for she had lost all interest in travel. It was merely a question of moving one's feet up and down, and marking time, and allowing the relentless places and anxious faces to do the rest.

In the end they had to come to you, otherwise, there was no point; if there was any point in anything at all.

She dipped into her deep handbag, brought up her bottle of Oblivdexital; then she stood still, inclined her head upward to the pock-marked canvas of sky, and swallowed two pills right down. And she looked not at the moon, because that would have been extremely unwise. And she looked not at Nelson's Column, for that would have been extremely unlucky, so she looked instead at the thirty-foot horizontal advertisement of a nude man and woman, and a nude bar of soap.

She wished there could have been an airship, a silent dirigible to come down to her, to her alone. A vehicle to lift her up, and hold her safely and lull her to slumber, to rise up out of these black dominions of death, to whisk her up higher and higher, as high as speechless joy, up into the plains of peace, those fields of golden love beyond the jaundiced eyes of the tearful stars. And further, and further. Beyond even the dreams within you. Up and up until the whole past was exploded; the whole dark dying congealing body was shot away, and you broke through the surface where you left self behind, and you floated until you found the end of the sky, and a way out of the sky.

'If only I could find the exit,' she said.

'If only I could find the way in.' His eyeballs rolled lasciviously, then, 'Can you slow down a little, Gloria, you're going far too fast for me.'

And she thought she was going ever so slowly.

'Doesn't London swing though, balls and tits and bums?'

'Do you have to be so crude?'

'I'm very sorry, Gloria. Please forgive me.'

She nodded. 'How can a city change so much, so fast?' Gloria noticed that now there were many more creatures now scurrying near the vast Trafalgar junction, and every creature seemed young and was dressed differently, and every creature was so much the same. 'Instant people! Instant characters! They just think you have to put the clothes on, and, presto, you're a handsome beautiful mature individual. Balls, Parsival! And I do not apologize for using it. There's been no revolution, no change. These are the new conformists—the danger, Parsival, is what they purport.'

'They call themselves ... New Left ... or Third World, or something.'

'Tosh! New Left, Old Right, Third World indeed? I'm still looking for first world. Have you seen it by any chance?'

'Where are the yeomen, the yeomen of England,' he boomed in a false baritone.

'There they are, there's been no revolution.' She swept her arm around the sky, denoting all the furry, hairy, starey, starry-eyed kids passing by. 'We're all the same inside. Afraid and ridiculous, alone and waiting.'

110

Parsival started sniffing again.

Perhaps that was the way he got his kicks, he was a smell freak. Still, rather that than trying to grope her flesh with eyeball or claw. And when she breathed in she was not relieved. That reassuring smell of sea weed had been blanketed out by Aftercum and Fanny Fresh.

The hospital stood just across the road, and she was coming back, down to earth, which was perhaps just as well. A particular boy and girl stood outside the post office, or it could have been two boys or two girls. 'Excuse me, darlings, where do you come from?'

Their mouths dropped open. 'St Albans, why?'

'But haven't you heard? The whole of Hertfordshire has been destroyed.'

Gloria strode away from them without waiting to see the effect. And she could have sworn that there was this roaring of animals, but she reassured herself with the fact that Charing Cross, where she was standing, was miles and miles away from London Zoo.

14

Midas tried to reach up towards her. She was pleased when he failed and had to ease himself backwards on to the pillow, in slow motion.

He groaned, and then smiled. 'Who are you, dear lady? And where do you live?'

'Midas, it's me, Gloria. Gloria Gaye!'

'Holland Park. That's nice. Just jot down your phone number and I shall contact you later. I'll give you a private consultation,' he winked his yellow eye. Midas was all yellow. He was shot right through from his fingertips to his eyeballs.

She wanted to get away from the jaundiced body. Perhaps if she fainted that would be a way of not having to face this horrifying obscenity of death.

'How nice of you to come. I'm going, Gloria, returning to the Cosmos.' Then he managed to fix upon his acolyte. 'Don't let the religion run down or fall into disrepute, Parsival.'

The yellow spores of death were floating everywhere. You could smell them; the combined smell of carbolic and mustard.

'I've missed you so much, so much. Who did you say you were? For God's sake, no cremation. No cremation.'

She could see the worms turning yellow, as yellow as his eyeballs.

'When I was born, in the beginning, I took one look

at the world, and saw that it wasn't good. And I loathed it, I tried to change it. But somehow I think I failed. What do you think?'

Parsival just shook his head. It's just as well he wasn't a professional actor. Dear Larry would certainly need to look to his laurels.

'Have I failed? Have I, Gloria?'

'On balance—I should say—it's touch and go. It's too soon.'

'Thank you. What a pity we never met. I'm going, tonight. Keep an eye on my religion, Gloria. I have been crooked, I know, I'm honest about that. But Parsival is crookedly crooked. I don't know why I ever took him on.'

Parsival was weeping. His tears were seeping into the sheets. 'Oh Father of the Sun, I shall bury your earthly remains in Willesden, as I vowed to you on a previous occasion.'

'You'd better, because I've made arrangements with a few of the boys, they promised to carve you up if you break your promise. And remember, only tiger lilies, bought only from Moyse Stevens at Victoria Station, or else. I want everyone there, all the old faces; all the old fingers. I want it to be nearly as spectacular as Winston Churchill's.'

She tried not to look at the face. At least traffic lights had the decency to turn green and red every so often.

'I know why I took you on, Parsival.'

'Don't speak, Midas, save your strength for your trip, oh Father of Ra.'

'I tried the Labour Exchanges, no go. I put an ad in the *Evening Standard*, only cranks responded. But suddenly I got a brainwave. I was at Southend-on-Sea

113

that day, so I phoned London. You remember, don't you, Percy Crouch, you were the only acolyte that the Alfred Marks Agency had on their books, so you had to do. Yes, I baptized him Parsival Crouch, didn't I, Parsival; only recently he lost his crouch, didn't you, Percy Crouch?'

'Yes Black Midas. You invented me. And I am truly grateful, oh Master.'

'As long as you never forget, Percy Crouch. Watch out! I may be a rotten friend, but I'm certainly a terrible enemy; and I'll get you, alive or dead, if you ever fail me and the creed I created specially for this world.'

The cancer spores were hovering in the air like pollen, and they were falling everywhere. She tried brushing them from her woollen scarf and from her eyelashes; but they quickly replenished themselves. And even the nurses were wearing yellow smiles now.

If only Black Midas would have the decency to close his lizardy eyes. Eyes, the cesspools of his yellow soul.

But he wasn't all ugly, there were parts of him that reminded her of Moss; the smile line from his nostrils to his lips, the crinkles near his eyes. He closed them, and for the first time she dared to touch Parsival. She clutched his wrist. 'I must go. I must get away.'

She tried not to breathe in. To inhale the cancer spores would be fatal. And then it dawned on her. Midas could easily have been the person who had stalked her ever since she had come out of that hospital. He was not here pretending to be dying, on the contrary, he had been dying for a long time and he was bored. He could easily have slipped out of the hospital to follow her on several occasions. And slipped back into his death bed without being missed. For if it was not

114

Midas, who was it that stalked her through the long night of the Metropolis?

She rejected the thought as far-fetched. It was unlike her to be so morbidly imaginative. It was unworthy of her clear and logical mind. There was Midas, dying nicely. He was still and silent, his body heaving gently as he breathed without sound, amongst the dancing yellow nurses of Charing Cross.

'I really must be toodle-looing.'

'Hold on, I'm coming with you,' Parsival whispered, then peered closely at Midas who seemed satisfied. They started towards the door.

'Percy Crouch! Where are you? Parsival, where are you?'

'Here, master!' Parsival dashed back to the bed and Gloria sat down. Nothing was that easy.

'Take down these, my last words, Parsival. That's what you're paid for.'

'Yes, Midas. I am here beside you, hanging on to your words. The whole world waits.' He stood poised, with pencil stub and an inside page of *Penthouse Magazine*. And the virgin stomach of a non-virgin pin-up awaited his scrawl. 'Does this follow your previous canon to the hermaphrodite philistines of the King's Road, Chelsea?'

'Just write, Parsival, and shut up. This is not for the world. This is private guidance for yourself and for your High Priests. Keep the religion, I beseech you. Keep it high-class. And spread out. Proselytize prodigiously towards South Kensington and Holland Park. Waste not your time in Kilburn, or in Chelsea or in Hampstead.'

So here was The Black Midas, lying transparent and incapable, with all his yellow blood visibly coursing through his veins, and all his cataracting flesh was melting into the mattress and the legs of the bed, that was biding its time before revealing its true purpose.

Gloria decided to take just one more tablet, to protect herself. She was sure that this would enable her to escape the yellow fever, and the fact that the tips of her fingers were already yellow did not unduly disturb her. When she left this place, one phone call to Mr Moss in Belton, or one to her daughter in Harrow, would immunize her forever from the cancer.

'I've seen you before,' the staring eyes of Midas said to her.

But she was safe now. She had given him the slip and there was nothing to be afraid of. There wasn't a man alive who could catch up with her. She wasn't even curious to know why he had followed her so endlessly whilst suffering with cancer of everything. Men were unpredictable beasts, you simply could not afford them. For a moment, she imagined she was with her lovely boys again. They were spectacularly sommersaulting and cartwheeling within the golden arc lamps.

But when she returned to the reality of the yellow room, Parsival was again trying to move backwards and away from the bed.

So she continued singing and gazed into the silver witchball in her living room. 'Someday, my heart will awake, someday the morning will break . . .' Gloria lifted the precious silver frame, where two cherubim held grapes for each other. She studied the tranquillity of the face, that precious sweet photograph, and those words in magenta, 'To Darling Gloria, with Everlasting Adoration. Ivor.'

The words were written with such beautiful calligraphy. The gods had no right to claim Ivor so early. 'I expect they were jealous of the loan they made us,

116

and wanted him back because he was on the brink of discovering the secrets of immortality; just another gift for mankind, to add to all those other magical qualities he had given us on earth.'

Tears splashed down upon his serene head, and before he disappeared, it seemed as if he was the one who was crying.

'I'll never let you go, Gloria. Goodbye for now.'

'Ivor, sweet dear Ivor, come alive again.' Gloria dabbed her eyes and soaked up her tears with Kleenex. The swish of starchy nurses replaced the lace wings of the angels, and the magical face of sweet Ivor Novello was replaced by the yellow obscenity of Black Midas.

'He's gone.' Parsival held a confirming mirror to the slightly open mouth. 'I'm dying for a smoke.'

'Remember what he said, no cremation. Willesden Cemetery! Fix it, Parsleyballs.'

She felt gay again because everything was slipping back into place. The tablets were having a marked and remarkable effect. That man would no longer follow her wherever she went. She was free again, she had not caught the creeping cancer of the world; no one had touched her and she was clean.

Gloria was leaving the hospital; she was going towards a telephone kiosk. She was going to phone her darling daughter; she was going to give her a real piece of her mind.

15

Miracle! It was daylight for a change, and not only day, but spring. She knew it was spring, for although the sky still threatened, the crocuses were opening, irrevocably.

There was something to be said for the outer suburbs, but what that something was, she couldn't quite manage to bring to the tip of her tongue.

Harrow looked quite un-ugly, which was very surprising, for no one had ever mentioned the place without an air of hatred or cynicism, which really was quite unfair. For no doubt it was very nice for some.

Gloria breathed deeply God's fresh air, and decided to make the most of it, for this was probably the closest God would dare venture into London. He too was obviously afraid of the maze, and the maze and the minotaur were one.

The suburbs were a useful place; a handy jumping-off ground for the everlasting underground. Harrow could be very harrowing; if you were not Gloria Gaye.

'What are you doing?' It was a police officer.

'I'm rehearsing for death.'

'Are you lost?'

'Aren't we all,' but then she realized that she need not feel compassion for this outrider. It did not do to stoop down in Harrow in order to see if crocuses had the audacity to transmit perfume.

'I'm looking for my daughter,' she said, assuming the role of a Chekhov heroine.

'Don't expect you'll find her down there.'

She knew how to deal with policemen. You had to take a strictly nineteenth-century attitude. 'Do you know where Ferndale Avenue is, my good man?'

It worked like a charm. Either 'my good man,' or 'officer', or 'constable', would do, provided you pronounced the latter, 'cunstable'.

Gloria knew that he was giving her explicit directions, and she nodded, but she did not digest the words that went through one nostril and out the other. And he whizzed away on his pop-pop machine, happy in the knowledge that the sanctity of Middlesex was not going to be destroyed by a stooping lady in the early afternoon.

She was in no hurry to reach her destination, so she wandered and stooped through leafy avenues and laurel crescents, stopping and stooping every so often, noticing the encroachment of spring.

'Spring is coming, tra-la-la! Spring is imperceptible, inexorable, irrevocable, spring it seems is inevitable, for nothing can stop it now.'

If the world suddenly discovered the neurotic middle-aged woman, and she had the opportunity to record her song, she had no doubt it would go to number one in the charts. Even if it was a little Japanese and high-pitched. The world needed to get used to new sounds. After all, the old sounds hadn't accomplished very much. They had not cured cancer, nor put back together a broken heart, nor negated the horrors of nuclear fall-out, nor silenced and made tender a thankless daughter.

Gloria was going to her, and it was just too bad. Angela in her deodorized paradise would have to realize that neurotics were not sick people. Indeed neurotics

119

were the first prophets of sanity. For who in her right mind would accept the madhouse of the world? Only Gloria Gaye and people of her calibre would dare to look into the mouth of the monster, and know that the sickness and the stench of the sickness had to be eliminated.

It was a pity that spring flowers hardly had a scent. One day she would go into a wood and look for violets. Violets, she remembered, had a definite violet smell. Mr Moss would come with violets, and Mr Moss would come soon. His coming was as imminent as the third coming of Christ.

All Harrow stretched before her on its back, in a quiet agony of expectation. Waiting for the coming with legs wide apart; silent and breathing deeply. For beyond the rattle of milkbottles and the hushed tiles in sanctified supermarkets, there hung the certainty of that coming. It was written as indelibly as spring, and nothing could stop it now. The irises and the lilies of doom were waving through the windows of the florists. She knew that it was near Armaggedon. And the house was near; that ordered pile of bricks where Angela her daughter shielded herself from the universe.

She stood by the door, and for a moment considered when she had been there before. No one was at the window, so she watched a pink hyacinth, and she knew full well that the no one in question was her daughter, who now stood by the open door, in the corner of her eye. 'Mother! What are you doing here?'

'You called me Gloria once. You know I hate that word.' She did not deign to acknowledge her daughter's face, but walked into the television commercial interior.

Only when she was sitting down did she speak to her daughter, 'Who was it, Angela, who said, "God gives us

120

our family, thank God we can choose our friends"?'

'What do you want?'

'I want to lie down, and go to sleep.' Gloria pulled off her shoes, stretched out upon the settee and closed her eyes. This was her only child, and it was just as well. And it was just as well that she went for months and months on end without thinking about her. Never in all her days had she experienced that feeling; that so-called maternal instinct. It had never fallen upon her like manna out of the heavens.

She looked at Angela. Tall she was, and thin, with little lemons instead of breasts. It was amazing how a person came through you and was such a stranger.

'When did you come out of that place?' The daughter handed her a cup of tea; yet Gloria could have sworn that she had only just arrived, and there hadn't been enough time.

'A few days ago, I think.'

Angela sat near; as near as Gloria ever wanted her to be. She hated contact with any part of her daughter's body. She had never been able to stomach the smell of her. It all reminded her of him. Sean! The one marriage of her life. The one true disaster.

But that had not been the reason; the reason why she had not come. And this impossible daughter of hers was also nothing to do with it.

'Angela, why were you so desperate for respectability?'

'Perhaps for the same reason you were so desperate to avoid it,' the so-called flesh of her flesh replied, and made her flesh creep. And thinking about creeps lead her logically to her next question. 'How's Timothy?'

'He's—well—' Angela cut herself short. It was as if she was about to pour out a diatribe upon the absent head of her husband. And she seemed disappointed that she was unable to follow her desperate desire.

'Has he still got weight problems?'

'Timothy is Timothy!'

As far as she could remember, Timothy did have a weight problem, and an ugliness problem, and an umbrella problem, and a baldness problem, and a heart problem, and a smoking problem, and a penis problem. Also a promotion problem, and a redundancy problem. 'Does he still have problems?'

'No he's given them up. He's quietened down now.'

It had been years, but her daughter had not changed. That's why people moved to Middlesex. It was a way of preserving the middle years of their lives; it was a form of pickling. The burnished shape of her daughter sat beside her; the capsule that had come into the universe via her uterus. But Gloria knew that the years had not stood still. And although she did not want to think about her grand-daughter, the child nevertheless loomed up in the darkness of her mind. And she lit up the whole universe, until stringed instruments played so beautifully that they lulled her into a niceness.

'You shouldn't have left Belton, you're not well enough.'

'I'm perfectly all right. It's you who are sick.'

'Mother, I don't know why you came here. You should have stayed in that hospital.'

'I have not been in touch with you for years, and when I leave, I shall not return.' They were eating toast now, and peach preserve, and all the tinkling sounds of the suburb invaded the lutes within her head. The ice-cream man came delivering his cones of death. The milkman, the oilman, the postman, the electric man, the Prudential man. The only trouble was that none of them were really men, and never would they be. Men

122

were extinct, but there were still a few women to be found, here and there.

Karen would now have been eight, or ten, or twelve years old, if she had not died so tragically. It did not bear thinking about.

'I'm afraid—' but then she continued. 'I'm afraid —you do not understand.'

'But, Mother, you don't need money, surely. What do you want?'

'You're afraid I've come for something. Well I have, I've come to ask you a favour.'

'I've got nothing to give. You should have stayed there.'

'I was a voluntary patient, I stayed for as long as it was necessary.'

'Please go back! They phoned me, they are anxious.'

'I didn't come to argue.' She knew what her daughter was thinking.

It would only take two signatures, one bribed doctor and one decaying relative, to have her certified. Why was it that your next of kin always reminded you of your mortality? Of your guilt? And your inadequacies?

'Nothing on earth will ever get me certified. I'm saner than the whole of Middlesex. Don't you ever dare to think of it.'

Angela looked angelic enough. She had given her that name in an attempt to force the angels to sit up and take notice, and bestow upon her union their own sweet benediction. It didn't work. Lucifer obviously recognized his own, and he had taken great care that the child should not fall out of his sphere of influence. 'Angela, you're a monster.'

'Mother, you are sick. I'm very busy, please.' All the

while she had been polishing and dusting because the middle middle middle-class were so afraid of dust, in Middlesex.

'Your father saw through you long before I saw through him.'

'Which father are you talking about? My real father, or the fathers of your imagination?'

Gloria could have slapped that cheek and sent her daughter flying through the wall, but all she wanted to do now was sleep.

'I can afford you, Angela. I can afford one little non-event in my beautiful, bursting life.'

'Nothing ever happened to you, mother. Come back down to earth.'

'Oh, and what about my past? The one I wrote about?'

'There was never a past. Face it. Not anything you could write about. Just a little suburban past, and a breakdown after the change of life, and Daddy's death. A cliché existence, you might say. Come back down to earth, and grow old gracefully.'

'Shut up!' She stood, but decided not to stop smiling. The living dead hated the freedom of people who could really live their lives without patterning themselves on someone else; the living dead wanted to destroy all individuality; there was no depth to which they would not stoop in order to pull you down to their leucotomized existence. She did not wish to descend into polemics, for she knew it was useless arguing with a zombie.

But somehow she could not stop herself continuing. 'With reference to your father; you would like to think that you were not a bastard, but any one of those score of fabulous men could have shot you into me. Though how you could have come out of any of us genetically, I do not know.'

124

Angela had the audacity to pull her face around, so that they were breathing on to each other. 'Mother, you need a nurse. Or you need to go back there, please! Please let me call them.'

'You can't get through, I've tried. No one can get through to anyone any more. I've tried! I've tried!' Gloria walked away and upstairs to where she remembered the spare bedroom was. 'Do you mind me lying down? I feel so tired.'

The face smiled above her. It was not too unkind, no one was beyond redemption, not even her daughter.

'It's just that you never got over the death of him. He died too soon. It wasn't fair,' the face said.

'What on earth are you talking about? Please go away.'

'I don't blame you for inventing a past, in a way. But it's not good for you, Mother. We've talked this out before. Please let me get you some real treatment. I discussed this already with Timothy when I heard that you had left. There's a place in Oxford; it's very nice.'

She could hear her daughter going on, her words all hitting the same tone. But Gloria was floating now, and feeling beautiful and young, so she did not mind the fantastic things that her daughter was saying. She just let all the words wash over her like a gentle lapping sea.

'It was after the menopause—'

'You mean the womenopause. Men, I hear, have the change of life, but it merely leads them to more and more erections...' She slipped away again, and submerged herself into the gentle song of the lone bird, outside on a newly opening tree.

'And that book, I went along with it. You needed

it. But what's wrong with being middle-class and suburban? What's wrong with peace and quiet, and a family?'

Gloria felt very sorry for her daughter, and a wave of compassion broke over the whole shore. She just simply had to say, 'Even if you were born into the turbulence of theatre, even if you did have a predilection for the suburbs, I did what I could. And incidentally, if you say I invented my past, how do you account for my present? The house I own at the Seven Dials? In Holborn?'

'It was just as well Daddy did own property. Look, Mother, people have done many worse things. Come back down to earth, stay here with us and bury all your fantasies. Let's get you some proper medical attention, and soon you'll be your old self again.'

'I was never old, I was never myself. You don't understand.' She did not want to think of two specific things, but sometimes it was impossible to keep certain nightmares from the mind. The impending eviction, and the face of her dead grand-daughter. She did not want to mention her dead grand-daughter, for even though her daughter had been so desperately unkind, there was no reason to pay her back in the same coinage. Anyway, she was stark raving mad and needed help.

'I'm so afraid. Please let me stay here.'

'Of course.'

'But only if you stop feeding me your sick ideas. I will take anything, Angela, except you foisting upon me a suburban past and a loving husband who died young. You must not take away my beautiful passionate and fabulous past and leave me only with the change of life as a crossroad to my womanhood, to my humanity, to my desperate need to be free of being nothing. I must mean something.'

'Just sleep, Mother. Sleep.'

'Let me stay for a day or so. I'm going to be evicted.'

The daughter was at the door with a thin smile that was slowly dying. It was she of course, who would need to invent a past. It was her husband who was dead, even though his body went up to the city every day. Most human beings needed vicariousness, she couldn't blame her.

'I can't stop myself thinking about Karen. How beautiful she was. How old would she be now?'

Angela knitted all the time, she was now knitting her brow. Who was she knitting for, now that she was surrounded by the dead? She was knitting an expression for the face of her dead daughter, so as not to face her. One could not blame her because that little girl should not have died. No child should ever die.

'Karen's getting on for nine, and she'll be coming out of school in half an hour.'

'Yes, yes.'

Angela had never faced up to the death of the child. But who could? Gloria had been able to face up to the death of Angela, but then, that sort of death was possibly easier.

'Now, when she comes, promise not to upset her.'

'Yes, if you believe in the resurrection she will come home for tea.'

She could see her daughter shaking her head; soon she would have to leave her, because there was no way of helping her. She had no right to jolt her own daughter into reality. Who was there to say that reality was so wonderful? If you took just one look at the world, you could not, in all honesty, commend it. They killed people in jungles and in cities, in reality. They smashed their brains in and shot them, in reality. They shot them through the back of the head and into the mouth, in reality. No, reality was really a dead duck. It had had its time, and it was good riddance to bad rubbish. Reality had ruled like a tyrant, and had had its way too long, and everywhere children were dying. In hospital wards and in villages. And they were being born maimed and crying. And hungry. They were swelling up with hunger. Calcutta was reality, and so was the Hospital for Sick Children in Great Ormond Street.

'Angela, I can't blame you.'

'You rest now, Mother, we'll work things out.'

Gloria had to admit that her daughter was a brave girl. That had come through from the past. Angela had inherited a little bit from each of those fabulous men. And had she not hated her daughter so much, she could have loved her.

Angela tiptoed out, and down, and no doubt was polishing surfaces for the non-arrival of the non-existent non-daughter. And Gloria floated above herself.

'Come down to earth,' she said. 'What's so wonderful about the earth at this time in space?' And she knew that as soon as the earth came up to her, and presented itself in some natural and less intangible manner, she would leave her bed of foam, and go back to the centre, to London. And she would forget about what could have been, and what should have been. And live only in the everlasting that is.

But still the face of her grand-daughter persisted. The floating, pale closed face of the child Karen upon the water. She could not escape from that face now, nor could she evade the knowledge of her impending eviction. It was all flashing, faster and faster, towards her.

'BUT I WAS A CHORUS GIRL. I WAS A DANCER.'

128

She rushed to her feet and screamed downstairs. 'I WAS ON THE STAGE, I WAS A CHORUS GIRL. DENY IT! DENY IT!'

'So you were, yes, you were. So what if you were? You were, for a short time before I was born.' Angela's voice coiled up towards her.

'I COULD HAVE BEEN A GREAT DANCER. WHY DO YOU ASSASSINATE MY PAST?'

'I'm baking a cake. We'll have some presently.'

'I WAS A CHORUS GIRL. WHY ARE YOU STEALING MY PAST AWAY FROM ME? READ MY BOOK, IT'S ALL THERE.'

'Yes, it's all there. But that's not the way it was, and you know it. Please lie down. We'll think about the future, presently.'

Gloria went back to the bed, and looked up at the ceiling. She could have sworn that she could see a crack appearing, and she decided to compose herself, just in case she was being watched by someone from above.

Poor Angela was out of her mind. It was apparent that those who could not look squarely at the past, had to pretend that they would be able to look at the future. Yet she felt only an enormous compassion for her so-called daughter. For even if the girl did live in a world of total fantasy, who would dare to judge her? Everyone was entitled to inhabit the world or worlds of their own choosing, and no one should dare to point the finger.

And even though she smelled burning, and wished that she and the whole house would be consumed in the flames, the well-mannered, quiet-licking suburban flames of Harrow, that was still no reason for turning off one's compassion.

16

'KAREN! KAREN! KAREN! KAREN!' An ambulance or police car or fire engine wailed. It was incredible, for even inanimate objects now cried for her dead grandchild. And birds screeched the name, and children calling their mothers in streets all called the name. 'KAREN! KAREN!'

And it was not really surprising, for the child had been astonishingly beautiful. It was as if she had never really belonged to us, but had merely been on loan. Karen had been borrowed from darkness; clutched out of the black, golden and throbbing and beautiful. She had sailed right out of the hungry dark, by some miracle; but she had been missed and so was sucked back into the black universe before too many questions were asked.

'Mother! Mother!' It was more human now, so she turned. Angela looked out of the car window. 'I'll run you to the station. Must hurry though, because I've got to pick up Karen at her school.'

Only now did she realize she had been running, but she did not blame herself, and she slowed only a little. She had hoped to escape but wasn't duly alarmed that the car had caught up with her.

'I'll drop you off.' The car now was alongside and Gloria realized she could not win this sort of race, so she stopped altogether.

'I bet you'll drop me off.'

'Mother, you need help. Go back to London and see your doctor. Please!'

'I have an appointment with a funeral; with a friend who from now on will be working underground.'

'Please get in, I'll be late for Karen.'

'I can't face it. This place brings it all back to me.' She remembered now. 'When I lost my parents it was the worst thing in the world, but when I lost my granddaughter it was even worse. I can't afford any more tears, it would hurt me too much.'

'Please let's go, Mother. You'll feel better in London, I'm sure.'

Angela wanted to get rid of her but she wouldn't blame her; not really. She obviously reminded her daughter too much of reality. Who could face such a tragedy?

'Please get in. Please leave us.'

'Look, I have plenty of time. Let's go to the school first, I would like to meet this ... girl ... of yours.' She wasn't really being cruel. She would force her daughter to face up to reality however much she feared it. It would be better for her in the end.

'I don't really want...' but then Angela stopped speaking. It was hard for her to come right out with the truth, that she didn't want her to meet the child, and thus force her into realizing that the child did not really belong to her.

'Look, Mother, you'll only upset her. Please, please go.'

Her daughter's face seemed kind for a change.

'Angela, let's all be nice and calm. Now, drive to the school.'

'Come on, in you come.'

131

Gloria sat beside her and did not gloat over her victory.

'Sorry, you're right. Yes, we're only going to pick up Karen from school. And I'm glad you realize she's well. Be nice to her.'

They drove though the grey-green belt, and all the earth was opening up, and upward-diving suède mums with swept-up hair were hurrying from doorways and into their throbbing minis.

'Yes, yes. We're going for Karen. We'll be seeing her presently, sooner than we all think. Don't worry your head.'

Poor Angela. Here she was in a car beside her demented daughter, joining in some ridiculous charade. But sometimes it was necessary to do things for the sake of those you loved, or ought to have loved.

'Her school's just around the corner.'

'Yes, Angie darling, let us go to meet Karen.'

Who could face it? Who could afford to take in that reality, of that beautiful child floating in a water butt. 'What a stupid way to die; drowned in a water butt.' She turned, but it did not seem that her daughter had heard what she said. She was glad.

And there in front of them was the spreadeagled sky, and Karen upside down, floating on the surface with her golden hair like the fingers of the sun; and her eyes open, looking alive with all the colours of the wings of a bird of paradise. A pale translucent water lily, floating upon the vast dark water lake. And she was drowned and dead forever; drowned because this stupid cow of a daughter had been a coward, and consequently had moved to Harrow because she was afraid of the universe. And she had become respectable and had settled down with her fat, bowler-hatted adding machine, and her corgis. And look where it had got them; to the senseless death of a darling child. A quick and ghastly death during a T.V. advertisement. The death of a child so beautiful, that one could only expect the worst would happen. Could anyone wonder that even a person like herself, Gloria Gaye, would have a minor breakdown under the circumstances? What with a daughter as mad as humanity, who was now going to pick up a child who no longer existed; and yet somehow managed to pass herself off as a fully-paid-up member of society, despite the fact that she was a lethal machine who was driving a lethal machine towards a pile of bricks and waiting dead faces. And for no reason in particular, except to pass the time between dark and dark, in a place called Harrow.

The face came closer, right up to the glass. It fell from the sky, it came right down upon her.

'Karen!' Angela said. 'Karen, this is your grand-mother, do you remember?'

'Hello.'

'Hello, Karen,' she decided to go along with the deception.

The girl was a pretty little thing, and it really wasn't fair to drag her into a fantasy world, but then you could not reason with such a wretched and distraught person.

The child came close, with her pouted lips, and although Gloria could not bear the invasion of flesh, she decided to bear it for the sake of Angela.

'Now we must really go home, Mother. But we'll drive you to the station first.' All Angela wanted to do now was to separate her from the child. She could understand. And she would respect that, and go along with it. In fact, it was quite a relief to be able to escape. 'Please, I prefer to walk now. Drop me here.' She did not feel safe at all, and she felt there would be a terrible accident. People in Angela's condition should not be allowed to drive machines.

Angela got out and the child got out. But Angela tried to continue smiling, although the emotion within her was moving against the attempted expression. Angela's face was a battlefield, but the child hadn't noticed.

'Will you go straight to the station? Do you promise?' The voice was pitched for a scream, but it was forced out in a whisper. 'I really must get Karen home for tea.'

'Look, Angela, it's hard for me to say this, but I wish you would face the truth.'

The daughter was trying to push her away, and to pull the borrowed daughter towards the car, but Gloria felt assured that there would not be a scene. There were too many people about, and one rarely read about eruptions in Middlesex during a weekday afternoon. She could speak the truth without exploding all suburbia.

'You see, Karen's dead.'

'Yes, Mother. Please come and see us soon, when you're feeling better. Take care.'

'I don't think it's safe for you to drive the car, Angela. I'll take this neighbour's child to her home if necessary.'

'Leave her alone, don't you touch her. Don't you dare come here and upset us all. Just go.'

'No, no I shouldn't have come. I shouldn't wake you all up. It was a mistake. I mustn't be late for the funeral.'

There was an awakening, apparently of the dead; for all the eyes of all the women in the windows were staring across to them.

And Gloria knew it was quite safe simply to walk away.

'Goodbye, little girl. Bye bye, Angela, thank you for having me.' She waved to the pretty but frightened and waving child. 'Ta ta, little girl, ta ta.'

She waved and blew kisses, and her crying daughter looked away. It was good that she cried now; that would bring her down to earth, and she would be able to drive the child back to her home, in safety.

It was a sad deception, for Angela might have chosen a prettier child. A child who looked more like Karen, and more her age. Not a child many years older than that most beautiful child in the whole world. How could she be a grandmother to a child of about ten or eleven? To a child who did not have golden hair that lit up the whole darkness of the universe?

The station turned the corner and walked gently towards her. Everything was gone now. The faces and the suburbs had slipped away, and the silent train came rushing towards her. It was just as well she was no longer a grandmother. Grandmotherhood had been a mistake and it was not for her, neither was motherhood or wifehood. People adopted these roles to finalize themselves; to give them some identity in the universe, to give them some flesh to squeeze, and a name to call, and a place to rest one's head in endlessness. She would not be finalized. Her end would not be inevitable. One need not accept the inevitable. Her life could go in many directions, and it was not too late for her.

She got into the empty train and was glad when it shot away from there.

It had been wrong of her to intrude upon her daughter's living death. Harrow was no answer. The

135

dead of Middlesex had to be left alone, to bury their dead.

The face of her dead grandchild floated in the sky. Every so often in the slow clouds, she would come and go, and Gloria knew that soon rather than later, she would have to face the inevitability of her destination.

And she also knew that she would never see her grand-daughter again; or her daughter.

She had to face this; however painful it was to know and feel the cold terror of reality.

17

'Only make believe, I love you...' She could see the cemetery now. But that did not stop her singing, and if people thought that she was off her rocker, that was up to them. Before, when people thought that she was slightly neurotic or even more than slightly, that was her problem; but now if people wanted to believe she was out of her mind, that was their problem. 'Only make believe our lips are blending, in a phantom kiss ...'

She could see the grey upright marble slabs. If you half-closed your eyes, it reminded you of an ultra-modern city, seen from afar.

She could not resist the urge, so she did it. 'Ghastly wig!' She snatched off her curls and hurled the wig up in the air. It sailed right across the railings and landed amongst the tombstones.

There would be no more deception, she could meet the world head on, in the short hair of her own. Anyway, grey was in, who cared? Besides, everyone knew that premature grey ran in her family. There was no shame in it, and even though no one had known, and even she herself nearly always forgot the wig, she was pleased, and she breathed more deeply and freely.

Gloria hoped that the young woman with the pram would not pass her, or even loom up close in her sight, because she did not know if she could resist the temptation of battering the child to death with any sort of blunt instrument that came to hand; or indeed, with her ready white knuckles. And she felt much relieved and happier when the woman with the pram crossed the road and went in the opposite direction.

There were now just a few old people in the far distance, and no one would come close before she reached the cemetery gate. Gloria had no grudge against the old, even though they disgusted her sometimes, and indeed she had no grudge against the young, or even the very young.

Sometimes one had to acknowledge the sad dreadful thoughts that drifted ever so slowly across the mind. There were certain paths that one should not travel, but there were certain paths that one simply could not avoid. But despite this she continued singing. For all at once the peaceful stretch of sky descending upon her would enter her and cancel out the dark cloud mountains within. It was all being blown away by the wind that seemed to be neutral in this affair, and the wind blew the song of a lone distant bird, which was perched on a stigmated cemetery tree, right into her very own ears. After all, if one felt compassion for others, if one was continuously being taught to love one's neighbour, why could one not feel compassion for oneself? For all those neighbours within oneself? Compassion for oneself meant peace and compassion for the whole world, and the end of destruction; and the non-necessity for smashing open the face of the young child in the pram, by incessant blows; so that the whole past was fountaining blood and cancelling out all needs and all fears, and all dreams for the future.

She would not obliterate a child today; no, nor any day. And she also hoped that she would not need to obliterate any child by night; although she wasn't

138

promising herself anything, for that was as much as a human being could possibly hope to do, or not do, in this street which was curled over the crust of the earth, which was spinning endlessly in the lost universe of sickening endlessness.

'When you walk through a storm hold your head up high, and don't be afraid of the dark...' She tried to hold the tears back. But they gathered in her eyes and flowed out into the world, and she stopped singing.

The cemetery grass reminded her. 'Damn!' She had clean forgotten Mr Moss. Maybe he came, saw Edith, and had gone away in horror. 'Damn! Damn! Damn! Damn!' But then she saw the telephone kiosk. If she couldn't contact him at Belton, at least she could phone home and leave a message with that scrawny screech-owl.

It was dead when she tried to dial. It was dead because vandals had been at the kiosk. The wolves of Mammon had come with their nail-files, and ice-picks. And they had destroyed all means of communication in the world. Nobody could talk any more to anyone in the city. Yet it was only to be expected, and probably it had never really been different. There were only two sorts of people in the world, prophets and Philistines. The Philistine hoards were waiting at the gates to break into, and plunder, and sack the city. Some had already infiltrated, and were pulverizing and pulling down the city, with all its standards of beauty, and all its sanctuaries of peace. The demolition gangs of sleep-walking sub-humans were getting closer and closer to the heart, to tear it out, suck it dry, and burn it away into rising smoke. And all that remained were a few pockets of heroic resistance. A few prophets here and there, defending the heart against hopeless overwhelming, never-ending armies. The odds against them were

139

enormous. Nevertheless she felt proud to belong to that select few, no matter how hopeless the cause. For sometimes it was all worthwhile, even if there was no reward except the knowledge of the battle. The only glimmer of hope was the alive eyes of those occasional human beings that you came across, here and there.

And most of them would be here today, for the passing of Black Midas, who had fallen in battle against the mongoloids.

There was one individual less in the world today, and he was about to be lowered into the earth. But at least she knew that she would have the compensation of seeing a rare gathering of those prophets who had so far survived, survived through from the past, when people were people, and did not conform, or acquiesce amongst the legions of the living dead.

'Midas, I love you. I come with fresh flowers.'

The flower-seller was also borrowed from the beautiful past. For she and her basket seemed incongruous against the concrete façade of the main street that stopped just at the edge of the cemetery gate. The flower-seller was as fat as the barrage balloons that once tried to defend London. She hovered over her huge Victorian straw basket which contained the flowers. The flower-seller wore a Victorian smile, and the cemetery gate seemed quite an appropriate place for her to sit, for she had nothing in common with the High Street, nor with the glassy glazed housewives of Willesden where this cemetery happened to be.

'Can I help you, luv?'

'Please. Can I have some beautiful blooms for the passing of a great but unknown prophet?'

'Yes luv, 'ow about irises. Messengers of the Gods! That's what the name means.'

'Thank you, but no thank you. How much are the lilies?'

'The Arum lilies are dear, but they're lovely. Seventy-five new pence a bunch.'

Gloria counted each white trumpet bloom. 'But there are only ten in this bunch.'

'Oh yes, luv, it's a continental dozen. But they're ever so fresh. They smell beautiful, don't they? You can't beat Arums for a passing.'

'Wrap them up.' Gloria gave the fat old cow a pound note and took the bunch.

'It's a bit chilly, ain't it?' The flower-seller with the red face against the white concrete world smiled as she gave a little shiver.

'Yes it is, it cuts right through you.'

Gloria left the world and entered the cemetery. She did not have to ask anyone the way to the grave, because she could see a clump of people exactly ahead, amongst the wildly waving trees. It was a very reassuring sight.

'So everyone came. Nobody let poor old Midas down.'

All those incredible individuals from her fabulous past were gathered to pay homage at the passing of a warrior in that everlasting war against inhumanity.

And now her tears were of joy, and she did not mind shedding them right out into the open, and spilling them upon the earth where snowdrop and crocus and primula were raising their pretty little heads. Despite all the darkness of the world, it was very comforting to know there were certain people you could rely upon, right to the end. Her own sort of people.

She noted the beautiful day as she walked towards them. Everyone was always stupid about cemeteries. For her they were comforting and gave her a sense of security.

She approached, but more slowly now, and could not believe that this crowd of alabaster faces, all clad in uniform black, were mourners for Black Midas.

She was relieved when she saw Parsival a little further on, just slightly beyond the unfamiliar group. And he seemed just as pleased to see her.

'Where's everyone? I understood everyone would be here.' She fanned her face with her hand to show the physical exertion the journey had caused her. 'So sorry I'm late, the traffic's awful.'

'At least you came, even if it's all over.'

'But where's everyone?' Midas had thousands of friends, and yet here he was, already buried, and nobody was there except this awful creature and herself.

'Great men are never recognized. Look at Van Gogh and Wolfgang Amadeus Mozart. At least Midas didn't suffer a pauper's grave. I saw to that.'

'Was the ceremony beautiful?'

'No, the Church of England insisted on putting their Christianity bit in. I'm doing the real part now.'

'Thank God he didn't suffer.'

'He suffered most awfully.'

'I'm so pleased. To suffer is the worst thing. And I'm so pleased it was a quick death.'

'He died as slow as a constipated snail, you watched it with me. And he's left me with such a lot of organizing to do.'

He turned with raised hands as if addressing a mass meeting. 'Oh Ra! Midas cometh! Oh Horus, hear me. Osiris, he seeks thee. Gather round, oh followers of sinful Seth, purge yourself of your darkness. Follow Midas into the immortal pastures of the sun.'

All the people at the other funeral turned from their gaping graveside, and stared; open mouths on stark faces. Their priest was absolutely furious. 'AS FOR MAN, HIS DAYS ARE AS GRASS,' he shouted, repeating himself, red in the face. But none of his gathering took any notice, they were all hanging on the words of Percy Crouch.

'Leave your nasty Christian heritage; we have a very fine religion to offer you, over here. And it wouldn't cost you nearly so much, in the long run. Our way is not the way of sexless self-denial, we say, enjoy the fruits of a passionate, all embracing, all understanding, ripe, abundant God.'

The mourners from the next door grave were becoming more and more interested.

'I shall see you outside the gates, if there are any amongst you who need a real change of life.' Then Parsival saw that the furious priest was about to explode, so he exploded himself.

'ADAM! First accountant in history! Turned over a new leaf, made an entry.'

They laughed. Some roared.

'I speak to prove that we believe in joy, and love, and laughter. Tell you more after. Come close, gather around, for now I must consign Black Midas to the sun.'

'AS FOR MAN, HIS DAYS ARE AS GRASS.' The priest belted it out this time. And he was going so red in the face, it seemed that he was ripe for a heart attack, indeed, about to burst. But it didn't seem to to make an impression upon his flock.

'Christian! Your days are numbered. Go back to your —' Parsival was about to say 'choir boys' but decided that this was possibly going a bit too far, so he quickly continued: 'Midas! What can I say of him? He was not all bad. In Ra, everything is forgiven, even the sins of Black Midas. The fact that Midas resided in Her

143

Majesty's Prisons for half of his life does not exclude him from Paradise. He also did some good in his life. Receive him, oh Ra!' He cried now. She could see him trying to taste his tears as they flooded down. Parsival would probably build up the religion very well.

She noticed that now the crowd was completely hooked.

Parsival threw himself upon the earth and wept bitterly, as he beat the ground with his fists. 'Oh Midas, Ra has his reasons, but why did you leave us? Let me come with you—'

He turned, inclined his head to the gawping group of mourners. 'You see, we are not cold and indifferent. I have inherited all this earthly sphere, I have become one of the richest men in the world, yet for what?' He pushed more tears down his wet face and once more embraced the earth. 'Tell them Midas, to take me. I want to jump in your coffin—Oh, don't hold me back.'

He looked around nervously, but everyone had taken heed, and no one was holding him back. He hovered, swaying on the edge. It was a pity that Hollywood did not send film scouts to cemeteries.

'Oh, I want to die, I want to go, to become immortal. Save me someone, save me from myself. Shovel earth upon me. Who am I? Where are we? What is—'

He was getting quite carried away and was carrying devotion perhaps a little too far. He watched the watching crowd, and there was now nothing he could do but jump on to the coffin.

'Oh Midas, I embrace you.'

She leaned down and touched him. In the other hand she held a fat stone that she showed him. 'I can crack

144

your skull open if you like, and save you from a fate worse than life on this earth.'

It did the trick. Parsival jumped up and she dropped the stone.

'Farewell, Midas, we the sad children of Seth salute you. Go now.' He looked to his audience, but they had dwindled back to their own hole in the ground, to their own frail priest who by now looked as pale as Christianity.

She was pleased things had returned to a sort of normal.

'Let the dead bury their dead,' she said.

Meanwhile, Parsival continued for just the two of them; or maybe three, if you could believe that Midas had been able to watch all this, despite the fact that he was so busy travelling his long journey to the sun. 'There you go, Midas. Later, later. There you go.' Parsival of the glazed eyes shook his head, and now realized that he had gone too far. So he came back down to the cemetery.

At the other burial service they had caught up with their schedule, and earth was flying through the air, and professional grave-diggers had taken over from the amateur relatives who were weeping their winding way from the scene.

'Don't forget. I'll give you full details at the gate. The enrolment fee is very reasonable.'

Parsival rushed after them, his eyes looking left and right, like a tic-tac man at the race course. He was obviously scared that some official would see him and enforce the probable by-laws of the cemetery.

Gloria stopped sniffing and was ready to go. She threw the flowers onto the coffin, and Parsival returned, stuffing his pamphlets and publications back into an inner pocket.

'Has anyone ever told you you stink to high heaven?' she asked.

'Yea! Often.'

At first she thought she would look for her wig, but then decided against it. She would return immediately to Soho, drink a few pink gins, and forget all about the past. 'Why didn't anyone come?'

'In the end you can only rely upon yourself.' Parsival plucked the dirty tear from his eye. Yes, it was possible that he was genuinely sad and lonely.

'You see, Gloria, my father-ship has gone. He has seeped back into the universe.'

She would not retrieve the wig, she could face the world as she really was, and the world would simply have to put up with it. And that was that. 'Yes, I expect they're all dead, all the old characters. Dead, one way or another.'

'Yea! All except you, and you turned up.'

Nothing stood in her way now. No one shielded her from the glaring dark, the great gaping mouth of the stinking universe. No familiar faces would help her in the fight against the everlasting legions of forever. No one would stand at her side; no one would fight with her. She was all alone, defending herself, and the world of diminishing light, against that ravenous monster called the universe.

Gloria walked back towards the maze of streets. A madhouse and a cemetery was no different from the world. You could draw a circle anywhere, and you had a madhouse or a cemetery.

Her awareness of the all-pervading dark somehow only emphasized her gladness at being alive; and she felt a sudden onrush of joy. She remembered her childhood and then could not hold herself back any longer.

She jumped upon a flat gravestone, and hopped and skipped from one gravestone to another. Stamping upon epitaphs, laughing, hooting. She had not played such an exhilarating game of hopscotch for years and years and years. And she did it with reverence for the twisted dead saint who had at last gone straight.

'Midas, you stupid bastard, I'm glad that you're dead and I'm alive.'

And she couldn't stop herself from poking out her tongue. And she so wanted Parsival to join in her leaping. No time had passed since she was a child. She could jump as high as the moon; as the sickle moon that had caught in the threads of the sky. She could leap as high as childhood.

'Yippee! It's great to be alive. You rotting stinking dead, it's great to be alive.' She poked out her tongue as she hopped. She poked it out as far as it would go.

Then she stopped her game because she felt their envy. She knew that if all the dead, of all the earth, could speak one line, they would shout in unison: 'WE ENVY THE LIVING. HOW LUCKY YOU ARE TO BE ALIVE, FOR EVEN JUST ONE DAY.'

And she had become so beautifully aware of her tingling body. The body was a dam. It was a capsule of translucent brightness. It was a tube of light, a vehicle of movement. The silhouette of skin held in life and kept out death. When you died, the silhouette was pricked, the vehicle lost all its light; and the silver sweet light of life flowed back into the black ocean of the universe; and the skin curled and withered away.

She left the gate. No one was waiting outside. Nobody followed her in and nobody followed her out, and nobody had been waiting there for her.

But Parsival was there, looking somewhat disappointed at his failure to attract even one customer from his recent audience.

'Can you give me a lift?'

'I travel by tube,' she replied.

'I hate long journeys, can I travel with you?'

'No, I prefer to travel alone.' She walked away from him, but noticed his reflection in the window of a shop opposite. He was now trying to sell his testaments to the fat old cow of a flower-seller. He was having a very hard time.

She walked away and entered the station. There was a line direct, back to the centre. She got her ticket and went down. She stood still, and yet she went down. And she waited on the platform. No one had followed her; no one would come for her, and she was glad.

No one, except Mr Moss, of course.

18

They looked so puzzled when she entered.

'It's me. Gloria!' she said. And then they recognized her.

'Congratulations!'

'Thank you.'

'You've seen the Diary then?'

'Who hasn't,' she replied, but still wondered what on earth they were talking about.

'It couldn't be better; just what we needed.' Oliver was red in the face from joy and booze, redder than usual.

Gloria sat down beside Jimmy, who pushed a double gin into her hand. Unfortunately he wasn't very clever as far as tonic was concerned, because he drowned the drink in the stuff.

It was a welcome change to be back in the French pub, especially after the cemetery. And Oliver and Jimmy were a sight for sore eyes. Jimmy offered her the newspaper.

'Bless you.' She took it and beamed him back a kiss. How could she have been so totally wrong about Jimmy? He was quite delightful, human and sincere, even if he was a journalist. He certainly proved the exception.

The print was drowning too; running right down the page. One day she would get her eyes tested. Meanwhile, she smiled as she looked at the coagulating mass of print, and the photograph which also was disintegrating into the sediment of the page.

'You did a fantastic job, Jimmy.' Oliver rubbed his white hands with over-emphasis, as if to bring them back into the world of the living.

'It's a marvellous story. You can always sell if you buy right.' Jimmy took the newspaper from her, and the two men poured themselves into it.

'So much space, and such a beautiful photograph. I'm sure the book will get a new lease of life.' The journalist handed her another glass, filled to the brim.

'It's done so already. We sold the serial rights this afternoon, Gloria. The phone's been buzzing ever since the story. And I've almost clinched a film deal.' Then he turned to the other man. 'You see, I also act as Gloria's agent.'

'Show me that!' She snatched the paper away, but it wasn't any good, the page was still blurred. But she knew by the ominous feeling inside her that the worst tragedy had occurred.

'No more worries now, Gloria, and when you're evicted, we'll rent a penthouse at the Dorchester.' Oliver giggled and she gulped down another and another.

'It's me—in the newspaper?' She tried to keep her voice down and hide the fear and anger. 'Is it me?'

'Who else? You're an incredible woman, Gloria; forever playing games.'

The dots had joined together, and it was her. Her full face had come into full focus.

'Where did you get the photo?'

'Oh, that woman who lived in your house; I told her you told me to collect it.'

'EDITH!' she screamed. Everyone turned towards her. There was a moment of complete silence. 'I never told you—I never gave you permission.' She lowered her voice again and quickly manufactured a grin.

'Of course you did, the other day. Surely you remember.' Jimmy was also smiling, but she could see his fear.

'I know you're so changeable, Gloria, that's why I got you to sign this little slip of paper,' he patted his pocket. 'I must say, you gave me such a lovely human story. Best I've had in years, I could have placed it anywhere.'

She wondered if the worms had already started to work on Midas. Would the ones within join up with the ones without, and would they shake hands? She laughed. And she noticed how relieved the two men appeared. They would get theirs.

'I predict that *The Passionate Past of Gloria Gaye* will be on the best-selling list within two weeks.' Oliver now rubbed his hands through all the golden coins sprinkling down his eyes.

'What did she tell you about me?' Gloria said.

'She told me nothing. You told me, Gloria. Edith just gave me the photograph.'

'I don't want my face in the newspapers!'

'Too late now. It's irrevocable. Thank God. And you don't mean it anyway.'

But Oliver did seem slightly concerned. 'Gloria, how many authors would sell their souls for just one inch of space in that Diary?'

She thought the glass would burst, because she squeezed it so hard. 'Read the story to me.'

All the faces in the pub had not stopped staring at her; all the eyes were boring holes right through her flesh.

'SOHO LADY DEFIES EVICTION,' Oliver read in his sickening plummy voice. She snatched the paper from him.

'Give it to me! Give it to me!'

She could see now. She could see only too well. The story screamed itself. 'EX SURREY HOUSEWIFE, GRACE GREENWOOD, OTHERWISE SOHO CHARACTER GLORIA GAYE, AND AUTHOR OF FICTITIOUS AUTOBIOGRAPHY, *The Passionate Past Of Gloria Gaye*, TODAY DEFIED AN EVICTION ORDER AND REFUSED . . .'

The whole world knew.

And that was that. The whole world thought it knew, and even though it wasn't true, it thought it knew. There was no escape from that. She felt unclean, she felt exposed and very cold.

'Surrey housewife? How dare they? How dare you assassinate my past—'

'Gloria darling, who the hell cares?'

The journalist was trying to move away, and she wished it had been an ice-pick in her hand, and not the clutched newspaper. She would have cracked the skull.

'I'll sue them! I'll kill you! Who gave you permission to print these lies?' She stood over him and knew she was screaming; though not by the attitude of the faces in the pub, who were merrily chatting away, despite her crucifixion. 'A housewife? I was never a housewife! Take it back. Tell me I was never a housewife. Please, I beg of you.'

Gloria could see it was useless, so she sat down and stared ahead in order to compose herself.

'Fictitious? Fictitious? Who told you about the eviction? It isn't true. It's all lies. Lies.' She turned to the publisher, to appeal to him. He was an honourable man; once.

Perhaps she was only dreaming that she was awake, and exposed, in front of the Gadarene swine of Soho. 'I feel unclean—you've covered me with the bilge and filth of lies. Let me go!'

He pulled her back; the journalist. 'Gloria, calm down. It all came from you. In this very pub. I have your own statement, in my pocket. You signed it.'

'Show me.'

He wouldn't, of course, and she could smell the sewers. All the manholes of London were open, and stench was pouring out; out of the eyes and mouths of all the turd faces that surrounded her. Now she had seen enough of that world, and she could not take any more. They could blithely take out your past, your true past, your beautifully interesting and necessary past; and they robbed you of it.

'I was never a housewife! I did have a fantastic past. Please believe me. The book is true. Tell me that it's true.'

'What's truth?' Oliver replied. 'If you think you're happy, you're happy. Anyway, who the hell cares? We can all do with some success, for a change.'

'Exactly.' The journalist stroked her lightly upon the neck, so she was hardly surprised when it brought forth all the snakes from out of her mouth. She hurled the liquid from the glass, at him. It was probably better than smashing the glass into his face, and gouging out his shitty eyes.

'Edith! I knew she'd do something like this.'

'Gloria! I'm sure we'll sell the film rights. You'll be rich.'

'I was, until now.'

Oliver was pissed, but third-rate publishers were always alert to violence in the atmosphere. 'Where you going, Gloria?'

'I'm going home.'

She wished she would wake up. The relief would

have been so beautiful, but facts had to be faced. There were many things she had to do in order to wipe out the disgraceful revelations of a phoney past.

'Let's have some champagne. Why are you going home?'

'Actually, I'm going to kill Edith.'

She laughed as she swept all the glasses from the counter. That shut them all up. And she hurled one empty tumbler at the publisher, just for good measure. He ducked under his elbow, and she felt sorry for him, for it was a sort of humiliation to be showered by confetti of glass.

They were pathetic creatures, all of them. And all prepared to believe the lies of their world. All of them were unable to acknowledge the loneliness of human existence; the aloneness of it all.

She felt sorry for them, and she decided to walk home, very calmly. And she would deal with Edith coolly and mercilessly.

Gloria left the public house, and walked through the wind, grateful to be given, at last, an opportunity to be herself. She was in command of her destiny, and she had the power to create a fabulous, great, crashing crescendo, that would shake the very world.

'EDITH! I'M COMING! EDITH, HIDE, HIDE, I'M COMING. I'M COMING.' She shouted right into the mouth of the wind, and shouted with all her might, in order to oppose it. 'EDITH! EDITH! I'M COMING.'

But again and again, the wind hurled it right back. However, when she reached Cambridge Circus, there did come a gap in the long howling, so she screeched with intensity, as if caught up in a coronation of cheering, and this time her cry shook all the houses and ripped the jagged sky. 'EDITH! I'M COMING TO KILL YOU!'

19

She turned around. If somebody had been following, he certainly was most clever at darting into doorways and disappearing in a split second.

Anyway, this was the one time she felt no fear whatsoever.

She crossed the road and walked straight over to the crowd standing around her door. 'Are you looking for Gloria Gaye?'

The television man was already packing away his hand-held camera, but his eyes immediately lit up when she spoke the name.

'Yeah. Why? Know where she is?'

Gloria contained her vipers. 'She's over in that café. She's waiting over there to be interviewed.' She pointed to the Come As You Are. The window of the café was also crammed with faces.

She walked right past the café and not a soul had recognized her. Though now she was sure someone was waving. And even here, at her own door, nobody seemed to recognize her. None of the open-mouthed children, not the Greek tailor who was crooked in body, mind and manner, nor the fishmonger, nor even Edith who was peeping out from above, through the edge of her curtain.

No one, until today, had seen her without the wig, which she had reluctantly had to sacrifice in the cemetery, in order to assuage those who gave orders to her pursuer.

The phalanx of journalists, acting upon her words, were already across the road dashing to the café.

'She told me to tell you she's homesick for the dead. She misses you all so terribly. So do hurry,' Gloria shouted after them.

'Thank you, madam.'

'Thanks!'

They were gone. And the nose-picking children were gone, and the passers-by were gone. Gone, just like vapour. She stared up at Edith and smiled, and saw the terror of the eyes, before they withdrew back into the interior.

'EDITH! I'M COMING! I'M COMING UP FOR YOU.'

She was inside now, and slowly climbing the stairs. And she felt wonderful, despite the salt taste in her mouth. 'EDITH! YOU TOLD THEM. I'M COMING TO KILL YOU, THE WAY YOU KILLED ME.' She shouted each word slowly and separately. And as she ascended she remembered Gloria Swanson in *Sunset Boulevard*. 'Now, that was a performance.'

And she recalled the pyramids of Ancient Mexico, and the High Priest climbing slowly up to the shaking victim, holding an obsidian knife.

'The heart had to be cut out, and clutched, and held high to the heavens, and it still had to be beating, Edith.'

Gloria stopped at the kitchen, lit a cigarette and searched through the odd utensil drawer. She was fortunate to find the very thing she had in mind. The long meat skewer.

She drew the smoke deep down into her lungs and steadied herself. There was time. Edith was not going anywhere. 'Except you know where.'

This was just between the two of them. Herself and the lady from the Min of Ag and Fish. It was time to go to her.

In the room she could not see her, but Edith was there. That distinctive smell of clove, fishcakes and camphor balls, always clung to Edith's person just like a cloud of invisible flies.

'Edith, I've come to kill you.'

The reply was a heavy volume of silence.

'Edith! Come out from behind the curtain, I've come to kill you.' She spoke softly now, so as not to frighten the woman.

Edith's face popped out, and then the rest of her. 'Hello Gloria, what do you want?'

'Actually, I've come to kill you.'

'Oh really?'

'Yes, with this ... meat skewer.'

'Oh dear, I was ... just ... going to pack.'

'Don't bother about that now. You won't need a case where you're going.'

'But you see, I'm leaving tomorrow.'

'Actually, you're leaving right now.' Gloria lifted the skewer ever so slowly, and wondered where to plunge it to get the very best result.

Perhaps upward from under the rib-cage; up into the heart. Or possibly into the stomach and squish it around. But there was no need to worry, love would find a way.

'But why, Gloria? Why do you want to kill me?'

'Because I hate you.'

'But why? Why do you hate me?'

'It's very easy to hate you, if you're me.'

'Oh, I see ... oh ... I was just going to pack.'

'I'm sorry I hate you—I just do.' It was all very nice and reasonable, and it all sounded rather like a Fuller's teashop over coffee and scones. 'You see, you tried to destroy all my past. You tried to expose me to the world. I didn't like it, therefore I must drive this meat skewer into your brain. I'm ... so sorry.'

Gloria plunged forward, towards her frail friend. 'Come back. Come back! Where are you? Edith!'

Edith was gone from her grasp, who would have thought that Edith was so slippery?

Gloria lay upon the floor, hugging Edith's threadbare dressing-gown. 'Come back, Edith. Come back. Come back and let me kill you.'

She rushed out of the room, just in time to look downstairs and see Edith going out of the door.

'Come back. Come back, I say. Come back and let me—' This time she screamed and screamed, but it didn't do any good.

'EDITH!' She shouted out of the open window. The thin skeleton stood on the other corner hugging her bones. 'Edith, please listen. Do me a favour.'

'Gloria, how can I help you?' Edith called back. 'I'll do anything, anything,' she cried.

'Good! Just one little favour. All I ask. Get run over by a bus in Charing Cross Road. Get run over and smashed—Goodnight.'

All she wanted to do now was laugh, so she closed the window, and she laughed. The sight of Edith running along the inky street, dressed only in a long flimsy night-gown, was surely the funniest sight in the world. Gloria laughed and laughed against the glass, until she grew very tired of it all. And then she slept.

She knew it was a dream, because people simply didn't have such incredible luck. It had to be a dream, for here was Edith lying dead in Charing Cross Road. She had just been run over by a number 24 bus. But the fact that she knew it was a dream did not in any way destroy her pleasure. Edith's performance was as good as the real thing.

There were the usual spectators, and the bus driver, the conductor, and the stationary bus. The driver and conductor seemed glad for the opportunity of a quick smoke, though a few silently irate passengers were already running along the empty road to get to the nearest bus stop.

'Please let me through, I'm a relative.' Gloria pushed to the front of the scrum of people, all eager to see the corpse.

'Where was she going in such a hurry?' the child in uniform asked.

'Oh, I expect to the police station. You see, I was after her with this meat skewer. I was going to dig it into her brain.'

'I see,' replied the policeman, jotting it all down.

Her pussy was showing. Gloria didn't like that. Edith's pussy was winking at her, and at the same time it was oozing blood. 'Curse it! There's blood coming out of her pussy; and at her time of life.' But nobody seemed to care; they simply stood silently staring and jerking up and down.

'Pussy! Pussy! Pussy! Pussy!' but then she remembered that Tutankhamen was safe, in Ethiopia, so she returned to the scene of the squashed face. The policeman had got onto his horse and was galloping off, and the spectators gave him a rousing cheer. Blood came gushing out of the hole that had been a mouth. It covered the whole road.

But Cambridge Circus looked just as gay as it ever

did. It was an area of infectious charm, and fortunately nothing had changed since the Great Plague of London, which had broken out ages ago, though so far it had not been officially announced. But one lived in hopes.

Gloria loved dreaming, and she felt remarkably safe, for now she realized it was only Parsival who had shadowed her. She laughed at herself for ever thinking it was Midas. Parsival's shadow covered the entire Circus. But there was no sunshine. He was standing high in the sky; his legs apart. He was bending down, smiling, satisfied that he had finally run her to the ground.

He would get a shock, because he had not reckoned on Gloria Gaye. He would get what was coming to him. He had taken over from Midas, but he was a nothing man from Wimbledoom. He had brought fantasy to the world. He tried to worm his way into women. He had followed her ever since she had returned, again and again, from Surrey; through that electric convulsive therapy called Southern Rail. He had followed her into that place, had stalked her there, and followed her out. But now she knew him, and he had lost his power. Consequently she could put up with the sky avalanching down on top of her, and the street. Or the room in which she stood, tipping towards her.

The dustcart came, and the dustmen were smiling and, oh, so very polite. Therefore, she assumed that it would soon be Christmas, for it was then that they came with open hands for their usual annual dropsy. But now they seemed keen enough with the job in hand.

'One—two—three, in it goes.' Like shanty men they had taken hold of the sagging corpse, and hurled it into the back of the dustcart. Edith got all ground up in the crushing equipment. It screwed her right in, round and round. She went into the apparatus and it was not unhomely, and certainly no worse than a pig going into the mincer at the corner butcher.

And off they went with the huge screw at the back of the vehicle still scrunching her up. And the hole in the face was the last thing to disappear into the hole in the backside of the disappearing dustcart, that was being scrunched up itself, and masticated, by the smiling disappearing jaws of Soho.

But the blood was still there, so she soared up into the sky, and hovered over Cambridge Circus long enough to see that all the hoses of the firemen could not wash it away.

The Thames overflowed, and everyone queuing up outside the National Film Theatre managed to keep a stiff upper lip, even though they were bursting into flame. 'KEEP THE HOME FIRES BURNING,' they all sang very grandly, and Gloria was pleased that even they recognized the immortality of darling Ivor Novello.

She felt famished, so decided that very soon she would wake up, for all that stood between her and food was the very necessary journey homeward. And there she would have a really big slap-up meal.

'LONDON'S BURNING, LONDON'S BURNING.' Who would have thought that blood was as volatile as petrol? No one had ever tried to run their motor-cars on blood; well, not actually.

The River Thames was running with blood, and the blood was spilling over the banks and catching alight, but Mr Moss would come through it all, so there was nothing more to worry about, and nothing more to do except soar up out of the flames and zoom direct to her home.

Children danced around the maypole just outside the door, as all the fireworks of defence went up in waterfalls of smoke. And she flew down into her room, where she decided not to phone Elizabeth Taylor, because they were probably all full up on the yacht, anyway.

She stood in the corner for a while, to tip the house slightly towards her so that it should stand quite level and every step would not be uphill. She went down into the kitchen to stand before the new deep-freeze.

It had been immaculately delivered; and assembled, in her absence. She just stood there to admire it.

'Thank you, Noël darling.' That was very sweet of him, to think of such a lovely practical present, and for no reason at all. Why did there always have to be a birth, or a birthday, or a burial, as an excuse for a present? It was just like Noël Coward to do a thing like that. Or possibly it was sweet Louis MacNiece. He too was a real darling, and even death had made no difference at all to him.

Anyway, it was divinely thoughtful, whoever it was. She had always wanted a deep-freeze. And to her delight she now noticed that it was crammed to the very top with all sorts of frozen commodities. For instance, there was her daughter Angela, looking so splendid, and so delicately displayed. And there was her own dead husband, Sean, the one she had almost forgotten about, curled up with his ever open copy of *War and Peace*. He had never seemed to get beyond page seventy-nine. She snapped off a sizeable chunk of the corner of the book and chewed it. It was very nice, if you liked that sort of thing, and although marzipan tasted better defrosted, beggars could not be choosers, so she took the whole book out of his hands and ate the lot. She was also doing him a favour, and this pleased her, because she had often felt she owed him something.

And having paid her debt, she relaxed, and no longer feeling a sense of obligation, she pushed him over to one side.

And there was Karen. Her dead—her dear and very own grand-daughter. Asleep. 'Golden slumbers kiss your eyes, smiles awake you when you rise, sleep, pretty Karen, do not cry, and I will sing a lullaby.'

Tears fell from her eyes as she sang to the peaceful child. They fell upon the child, and they froze upon her, adding a layer of filigree lace. There she lay, her darling jewel of absolute innocence, surrounded by all the flowers and all the jewels of ice.

'Sleep now, and thank you, poppet. For now I do not have to face grandmotherhood.' She wanted to play back the deep-freeze, and looked at all the knobs, but was afraid to fiddle with them. So instead, she went to the Arum lilies, dialled her number, and spoke down them. 'Mr Moss, please come. Please come soon.'

This time a miracle occurred, he spoke right back down. 'Yes, I shall come down, soon, and take you back up with me.'

Out of the empty kitchen window she saw him climbing up the purple cloud, that forever seemed to hang overhead. 'Mr Moss, why do you go climbing mountains on a night like this?'

'I climb a mountain in order to see the next mountain that I must climb,' he said, or tried to say. It didn't come out that way. It came out as a song instead, and Julie Andrews' spring-cleaned lilt had been dubbed on to the voice of his now descended majesty.

But her eyes smarted, so she left the flower forests in the sky, and went back to the deep-freeze, to see how her little Karen was getting on. But Karen had been pushed to one side, and turned over, and sweet, dirty Black Midas lay before her. One eye open; one eye closed.

A sudden inspiration dawned upon Gloria. There might be a way after all, of earning a living.

It was obviously quite simple to mass-produce deep-freezes. The idea was not to keep food in them, but relatives and friends. Only those closest to you, of course. The ones you could trust. And what a boon it would be to mankind; to be able to take a peek at your nearest and dearest whenever you fancied. It was a most civilized idea, and far superior to stinking burial or crummy cremation. You could even keep all your ancestors from as far back as you liked, provided you had a deep-freeze large enough. 'Imagine! One's own family tree in one's own kitchen.' It was nice and proper to share your surroundings with your loved ones.

One could even possibly take them out for little strollies, every so often, and you could all watch tele together, and eat baked beans, and play flutes. You helping them all, of course. You could invite people in, and make them pay a small admission charge, and have a very modest sort of Madame Tussaud's of your very own.

Gloria was sure that the Conservative Government would welcome such an initiative of private enterprise. 'Joy, joy, joy. Things just get better and better.'

She hoped that they all recognized her joy at seeing them, so she waved at the deep-freeze again and again. 'Hello all.'

'Hello Gloria.' All cooed back, without moving a
164

muscle, which was very considerate of them.

She was pleased about this because if any of them ever did manage to become defrosted, even for a moment, there was a good chance that they would sign the certificate of death that would have her taken away, screaming and screaming and screaming, and screaming.

Gloria tried to put the lid back on the deep-freeze. Her stomach was grumbling, and therefore it was almost time to wake up. But somehow the lid wouldn't fit on properly.

Something was pushing it up again. Or someone.

It was Edith. She alone of all the occupants was moving, and actually coming up out of the frozen interior, and right out into the room; opposite her.

'Hello Edith. I'm ever so pleased you've come back.'

'Yes, I was simply frozen. And I've so much packing to do.' She pushed her bones forward. 'Here, feel me, I'm as cold as ice.'

'Ooh, so you are. Come over here, love, near the stove.'

Edith complied. She was very nice sometimes, and had her moments of co-operation; moments when you simply had to love her.

'Stand over here, Edith.'

'Where? Here? Will this do?'

Gloria tried to move Edith into the right position. 'Yes, just here, so that I can drive this skewer right into your eyes.'

'This better?—Ooh—This all right?' Edith shuffled into exact alignment, and she smiled and seemed much warmer now.

'You came back, Edith, I'm very, very proud of you. Here goes.'

She drove the steel into the eyeballs, one after the other, and it was done.

'Thank you very much,' Edith said as she went down, with all her liquids flowing out of her.

And Gloria knew it was time to wake up; especially as the door knocker was booming for her; booming through the entire empty house.

20

She let him go upstairs first, because she did not care to have his slimy eyes focus on her behind. She was not afraid of Parsival any more, she could face him; he could not touch her. Indeed, she was pleased to see him.

She had more to fear from the beasts of Fleet Street, and she had fully expected it was them at the door ready to pounce upon her, and tear her to shreds when she opened it. But for reasons of their own, they were not encroaching too quickly. She had cheated them by letting in the very worst that the fates could send, this ridiculous creature. It was laughable that he was the worst that they could send.

She wasn't quite sure if it was the day after, and then she wasn't quite sure which day before this could have been the day after. If indeed this was tomorrow. For still there was this extreme reluctance of light and dark to separate themselves. But this did not bother her in the least, as she entered her living room and sat on the floor. All time was one, and who in their right minds could believe that tomorrow would be any different from yesterday? Night was merely pushed upon the world as a palliative for man, in order to make him feel that things would improve the day after.

'I love it the way it is, I have no desire for change.' She moved to the cupboard that contained the piles of her book. Towers and towers of her past, untouched by man; clean. Her multiple lives all gently sleeping behind the covers within the towers. She started to take the books out, a tower at a time.

And methodically she split the books open and tore the bindings from them. When she finished this operation, she separated the pages and tore them into little pieces.

Parsival sat down cross-legged beside her.

'Edith's dead, isn't she?'

'No, I saw her, and followed her. She went into the police station,' he replied.

'So that's why you came, to tell me she's dead.'

'She's perfectly all right. So you needn't worry.'

'How did she die? I know, don't tell me. She was run over by a bus.'

'She is not dead. Edith is not dead.'

Why did they always imagine that they were telling you things for your own good? Why did they always need to reassure you? How arrogant they were. Why were they so afraid to come right out with it. 'What number was the bus?'

Parsival didn't reply at first, and then he changed the subject.

'What are you doing?'

'Tearing up my past. It was a number 24 bus, wasn't it? Going to Camden Town?'

'I went into the police station, having nothing to hide. They're taking her to Carshalton, to her sister. I spoke to her, they've probably taken her already.'

'Would you be an angel and help me tear some?' She pushed a pile over to him. He took one up and opened it. *The Passionate Past of Gloria Gaye.*'

'Help me, Parsival. I must have them all torn up into little pieces before they come for me.'

'Yes, they said they would come, the police.'

'They call themselves by many names. I can face them whatever the disguise.' She was pleased, for he was helping her with the tearing of the books. 'Too many cooks make light work, oh hum! I'm glad it was a number 24 bus.'

They both sat quietly for a while; and the only sound was the ripping of paper.

'They tell me I concocted my past, that I invented a fabuloso role for myself. I can tell you this, if that was the case, I would have concocted a far, far better role for myself.'

'They're coming for you, Gloria. What are you going to do?'

'They come for me all the time. But I send them packing, just the way I did with Edith.'

'There are crowds in the street outside, just waiting around. Can't you hear them? You're in all the papers. You're a sort of a heroine.'

'If it is a dream and we are being dreamed, who, pray, is the dreamer?'

'Any minute they'll come. Oh, they won't break their way in at first. They'll act in an English way; they'll try to coax you out. They'll come in uniforms and they'll have their own way. They always do.'

'Anyway, even if I had imagined the whole thing, would you blame me? So you followed her also, before she died. I don't blame you. You have your role in the gospels, however black and mysterious.'

'Mind you, I admire your guts. I like people who stand up for themselves.'

'So, I'm famous it appears.'

Parsival looked out of the window, and his face dropped.

'Are they ready to knock my door down?'

'They've all gone. Cleared suddenly. Not a soul. People get so bored these days. There's always something.'

She felt sorry that he was so greatly disappointed. 'I expect they'll be back very soon.'

A smile lit his face and she was pleased. Yes, they would come for her, presently, but they would not succeed. Nobody could move her, ever again; nobody but death, or Mr Moss, would make her leave her place.

They had killed the street, they had strangled it out of existence, they had boxed it up, and soon they would pulverize it off the face of the earth. But the heart would continue to beat. Her heart.

'Please, Gloria, let me help you. Come with me to my pad.'

'Just tear, Parsival, one inch squares, that's what I'm after.' He continued doing what he was told.

Now all the copies were spineless and coverless, and lay exposed upon the floor. Hundreds of copies, stretched right across the room; a ridge between her and the creature.

'She's better off though, isn't she?'

'Who?'

'Edith of course.' Why were people so reluctant to accept the reality of death?

'Yes, she's better off in Carshalton.'

'It's all getting very boring, let's change the subject. Why did you come here?'

He was doing his work well, she had to give him that. His little squares were very nicely uniform. But it was still going to take a lot of the dark of the day, or night, to finish it all.

'I've come with a proposition.'

170

'Spit it out.'

'I've come to share the religion with you.'

Soon he would go, and she would follow that part of her dream that had revealed itself to her. She would take up the bottle in the far corner; that little bottle of pills that seemed to be getting bigger and bigger, in that corner that seemed to be getting further and further away.

'Don't you want to have a share in my religion?'

'Tell me, Parsival, is Hitler dead?'

'Hitler? Hitler? Oh yes, Hitler. I'm not sure. Yes, I think he is dead.'

'Thank you. No, I don't want your religion. Why did you come?'

'To share the sun exclusively with you.'

'No, I don't want the religion, because I have to give you something in return.'

'You know what I want in return.'

'What do you want in return?'

'You know what I want in return.'

'No, Parsival, what do you want in return?'

'You know, Gloria, you know what I want in return.'

'Keep on tearing paper, you're doing very well.'

'I want you to invest a little money. You have some, I believe. We must invest in order to expand, we must expand in order to invest our love into a true memorial to Black Midas.'

'Oh, you want money?'

'Yes. I want—just a moment— Wouldn't you like me —us—to expand?'

She knew what he wanted to expand. His horrid capital growth between his crossed legs.

'You would like to be my partner, wouldn't you? Religions are booming. All I want is just a little something from you, now. Please give it to me now. It will make you very happy.'

What a toad he was. He cloaked his thoughts, he coded his nastiness. He could not even mention it by its proper name, but had to go through this charade. 'Money indeed. That's what you call it these days.'

His fingers stopped tearing the paper. 'Oh, do carry on, Plasticballs, you were doing so nicely.'

He came towards her, without standing up. He just shuffled across the floor like a cripple. He inserted a finger up into his nostril and seemed deep in dark thought. But one had to be thankful for small mercies, at least he had not tried to invade her own flesh.

'Why do you have to go, Parsival?'

'I don't have to go. I can stay. I can help you. We can branch out. Let me have it, Gloria, it's doing you no good locked away.'

'What a pity you have to go.'

She got up and looked out over the quiet rigor-mortis locked city. They pretended not to be there, but they were hanging around in doorways. Why were they all so afraid to show themselves?

'Pygmies!' How could you get all worked up about the little people who had inherited the world?

Again she thought of Moss, and wondered what was keeping him? And then she decided to telephone again, even though the instrument was a long way away. Possibly that cretin on the switchboard at the hospital had got it wrong, and there was nothing to worry about; because he was still there and yet to come.

She reached the peak. She had climbed up the room, and stood victoriously upon the summit. And even though she was a little breathless from the hard climb, this did not spoil her joy. But the phone was dead.

He took it from her. 'Maybe you didn't pay the bill, or maybe they've cut you off because you're defying them. It's dead.'

'It's not dead, it's only sleeping. Oh dear, must you go?' He stood amongst his little piles of torn paper, and then he stepped over them towards her.

'I want to sleep. I want some peace. That's all I want.'

He was a long time coming across the field. The little spider man in the bleak winter interior. 'I know what you want, I know what you want.'

'I mean, you may as well give it to me.'

'I want to lie down.'

'Playing hard to get, eh? So you're not interested?'

'I want you to go, and I want to sleep.'

'You need it. We could work so beautifully together. Let's start right away. You've needed someone like me all your life, I know it's what you need. I'm proposing this for your own good.'

'You filthy stinking wretch! That's all you think about. Men!' She swayed as she hissed the word at him; swayed so that he should not move an inch, just in case she bit her venom into his jugular. So they stood there; him smiling because he didn't know how to cry, or how to get down from the corkscrew scaffolding that he had built up for himself.

So Gloria continued staring through half-closed eyes. It was an expression that was in keeping with the hisses from her mouth. She remembered her Tuti again. You could stroke him sometimes, for an hour on end. You could lie down on the carpet, with him lying down upon you. Your faces almost touching; him purring deep down in his throat; then he would roll over, so as to receive the same therapy upon his undercarriage, his eyes all closed. And then suddenly his paw

173

would go out, like the tongue of a lizard; like five
tongues.

Like five tongues her claw went out to Parsival's
cheek, but unlike Tutankhamen, she did not merely
present the pads of her hands. Therefore her nails bit
deep into the flesh, and she pulled them downwards.

The middle rut was deep enough to draw blood out
of Parsival's skull, and thus proved that Parsival was a
living thing. And the blood ran over his fingers when
he held his cheek. He licked his fingers, and by the
expression of his face, his blood tasted good. To him.

'I must go now.'

'Oh, must you go now?'

'Yes, I really must go now. I've got a rather pressing
appointment.'

'Oh dear, you're bleeding. Thank you for helping me
tear up paper.'

'It was a pleasure. Pity you didn't want to help me
expand the religion.'

'Thank you for coming.'

'Thank you for having me.'

'Thank you for not having me,' she stopped herself
saying. Instead she went to the drawer and took out
five five-pound notes, and held them towards him.

He tried to take them, but she pulled them back.

'Who do I have to kill?'

'I just want you to come in the night, with screws and
nails, and planks of wood. And I want you to hammer
me in. I want you to do a good job so that they can't
get at me when they come; when that dark comes light
enough, in their morning. But you must promise to do
a first-class job. I want planks right across the door, two
inches thick and ten feet long, and nailed right across.

174

From the hoarding on one side of me, to the hoarding on the other side of me.'

'I couldn't do all that by myself, I'd need help.'

She took out two more five-pound notes, and he walked backwards out of the room.

'I need money for the wood,' he said. 'And the nails, and the screws. I need more money,' he said. 'Because it's night work, that means double time. And I want danger money.'

She took two more notes out of the drawer, and followed him, and gave them to him, and he held them together. And he so loved the wad, that he gave them his only begotten bloody, snotty kiss, before he stuffed them into his interior. And she descended with him.

'Where do I find a timber yard open, this time of night?'

'How do I climb the mountain again?' she replied.

'Bye bye, Gloria. We'll be running into each other.'

'Not if you're driving that hearse of a body of yours. I would hate to coagulate with you.'

He grinned his holes of blackness and slithered through the crack of the door. She was about to resume the journey upward, when he shouted. 'GLORIA! OPEN UP!'

She opened it, one inch. 'What do you want?'

'I hope you realize I'm breaking the law.'

'Goodbye, Parsival. Nail me in very well. So that no man can enter. No man, except you know who.'

His one revealed eye winked, and she closed the wood again, and that was that.

And when she climbed to the summit again, she once more took up the telephone; and it was true. It was quite dead. But the bottle of pills was very much alive, and humming, as it waited for her. And she knew that she and the contents were one and the same. They both demanded peace, and needed each other. Who was she to stand between the interior of one, and the interior of the other?

So she reached out, and her arm extended right across the wilderness of living-room. It brought back the bottle and she unscrewed. One by one she popped the pills into her mouth, and thus she and the world were joined in the holiest matrimony.

Then she continued tearing up the books. Smaller and smaller and smaller the squares were becoming.

And when she was done, hours or minutes or anniversaries later, she opened the window, threw open wide her arms and scattered her bounty. The white pieces showered down the black night, until they covered everything, for as far as sight. 'Confetti for the wedding.'

21

Everything was floating, slow; even the sounds.

'Gloria! Gloria!' The long-drawn-out call reminded her of someone, and of something.

She went to the window, but she could not see the seagulls. She searched the sky, but could not see the source of sound.

She pressed her face against the glass and watched the wind playing like a kitten along the streets. Probably the wind had been calling her. The snow was gone. All the snow that had fallen from her arms, and she saw Flora again; reflected in the glass. She was Flora; with all her beauty and all her sadness.

'Gloria! Gloria!' So it was a bird, an invisible prophet of dawn, singing somewhere.

'Stupid bird, haven't you heard the bad news.'

'Gloria! Gloria!' it called.

She threw open the window and leaned out. The sky was good for you; it was such a short cut, if you needed it. A quick way to eliminate all the faces she thought she had known. She would bear the sky in mind. You never knew when you needed a quick exit from a room.

And then she saw him. It was Parsival who called her name.

'Gloria! Gloria!' She could see her name coiling out of his mouth and rising in a bubble towards her.

'Gloria! Gloria!' It was a strangely beautiful plume of sound that Parsival was exuding.

He was waving, with a hammer in his hand. The planks of wood were on the pavement.

'Good Parsival, get on with the job I paid you for.'

'Before I start, I must have something to warm me. Can I come up for a drink first?'

He huddled and skipped up and down a few times, slapping his hands against his body.

'Just for a few moments.'

Day was a sly dog; it would be upon her before she could turn around. She reminded herself that it would be highly inadvisable to blink her eyes. She threw the key down, and closed the window.

When he entered, his smiling face started to expand until it filled the whole room. But she was sure that she wasn't afraid of him. 'Drink up and go.'

He drained the red liquid down, and did not take the twist out of his face.

'I'm very tired. Please go.' All she wanted to do was close her eyes, and all she needed was a little peace.

Everyone on this earth was probably worthwhile, even Parsival, and that was why she could dispense with everyone. An absence of everyone was so necessary.

She did not dare lie down until he had gone, but she just had to close her eyes.

'Why are you swaying, Gloria? Are you ill?'

'No, merely praying for an expiation of people.'

'Give it to me! Give it to me, you bitch!'

She was not altogether surprised when he grabbed her. She had known all the time what he was after.

But panic was out of the question. There was no salt taste in her mouth, and no speeding of her heart. There was just this creature, holding her and shaking her. But Gloria was not altogether astonished. She had had worse dreams! What was he saying?

'Let's stop mucking about. I know you've got it. You've got it hidden in the house. Everyone says so.'

'What do you want, Parsival?' She was not being calm merely because she was afraid to show her fear. Under these circumstances she knew that some people could resort to real violence, even murder. But still she was not afraid. It was probably her loathing, and her need for peace, that caused her a lack of anxiety.

'You know what I want. Money!'

'Oh, money? Yes! Come to think of it, I would have been surprised had it been anything else. It's only money you want.'

All she wanted was for him to go. It would be a fair exchange.

All he wanted was lousy money, and all she needed was precious peace.

'Give it to me! Give it to me!'

She pointed to where it was. To the sideboard. There were about ten fivers and ten tenners left in there. It wasn't a terrible price to pay. He could not really touch her real wealth, for that, like the integral part of her soul, would always remain untouched, waiting for Moss. 'Lay not your treasures up upon the earth,' she said.

But he was already bent down on the other side of the room, at the open drawer, pulling out all the letters, the official papers. And he had seen the bank notes, she could tell by the holy reverence in his sudden eyes.

Then the answer occurred to her.

She knew exactly what to do. How could one continue looking over one's shoulder? He had followed her for too long. She needed a rest from him; and while he lived that was not going to be possible.

He didn't notice her leaving the room; he was far too busy. Money was a very religious and emotional subject.

She went to the kitchen, for the skewer.

Parsival also needed a rest from himself. She would be doing him a favour, really. A petty criminal could only look forward to a horrible existence. Half his life would be spent in Wormwood Scrubs, the other half would be on the run; undernourished. She wouldn't wish that sort of life upon anyone, not even her worst enemy, nor even a dog.

She would be doing everyone a favour.

She tiptoed back and Percy Crouch was living down to his name. He was on all fours, practically, with the notes all spread out in a pattern around him; just like a child with a new jig-saw.

And she would be doing the ladies of North Kensington a favour. For it was not nice to live in a world of illusion. Besides, Parsival simply could not be rehabilitated while he lived. It would not be an act of sacrifice. And she had to admit, she was not doing it ultimately for the world, or herself. She was doing it for Percy Crouch.

He turned, but did not see the skewer. 'I want some more! Give it to me!'

'In there! In there! In that drawer, more in there!'

He shifted over on his knees. 'I want more! More! Give it to me! Give it to me!'

'I'll give it to you.'

One did not have to follow one's instincts blindly. She could poke out her tongue at fate. She could cheat the fates. She did not have to kill Parsival with the meat skewer at all. She took up the pair of scissors. 'There it is.'

180

His dusty claw had been reaching deep into the drawer when she plunged it; again and again, and again. Into his back. It was very easy. 'There it is! There! And there! And there! There! there!'

But he was most ungrateful and didn't thank her. And he stopped, completely.

He lay there, downward, so she turned him over. It was nice for all of them to get some peace at last. Percy Crouch had been rehabilitated and everyone could breathe a sigh of relief. He looked remarkably nice lying in his own blood; just as pretty and as innocent as a baby.

But there was simply no time for playing around. 'Heigh ho! Heigh ho! It's off to work we go.' She struck a high falsetto, carefully stroking the immortal words of Mr Walt Disney. And all at once she knew exactly what to do.

Remembering that it was chilly outside, she put on her vintage Persian, and then she dragged him. He came very easily. And all the way down the stairs he thudded after her, leaving a dribbling red trail behind him. But to no purpose, because he would never need to find his way out of the maze he was going to.

Downstairs, near the street door, there was a back-yard she hardly used. There was a huge green pram there.

So she pulled it out into the passage, and dusted it. It polished up very nicely, and she was rather proud of it. It was not the modern sort of pram, all wheels and no body that working-class mums in Camberwell proudly pushed around. No, this was a proper pram of the thirties; built for two children and a nanny; built to be pushed through St James's Park.

She dragged him into an upright position, and he fell against her.

'Do you come here often?'

She shook his head for him, so that he should not be rude to a lady.

'Would you care to save the last waltz?'

She nodded his head for him. He was most accommodating. She took hold of him, her arms all round him, and lifted him up. And there he was, lying like a baby. And she waltzed down the street with him.

Most probably they would come for her in the morning. But even vultures needed sleep, and no one was there. Nobody was looking down on her, and nobody was looking out at her. And nobody was looking up at her, and nobody was following her because Parsival was no more.

She waltzed through the Seven Dials towards that beautiful smell of rotting cabbages, for she knew the perfect place to dump him. Mr Crouch needed appropriate surroundings. He deserved such style and thoughtfulness, for he was a true acolyte, who was just following his master, Black Midas, out of this world of pain and darkness.

The banana warehouse was where it had always been; tucked away in the winding windy streets of Covent Garden; huddled up within itself, trying to keep itself warm to ripen its wares.

Gloria was glad she had remembered to bring the scissors, and she plunged them, not into his eyes, not into the lock, but into the old damp wood surrounding the lock. 'Amazing what you can do, when you set your mind to it.'

She entered the hall of bananas. All the hands of all the bananas, the green ones and the green-yellow ones, were opening and waving at her; welcoming her. It was a very nice gesture, to leave him there. The bananas towered above her, but nowhere was there one ripe enough to eat. And she was feeling quite peckish now, and homesick.

'Goodbye, Parsival. I leave you with enough food to see you on your way. Ta ta, be good! Don't go bad.'

It was far easier getting him out of the pram. She tilted it, and he slithered out and lay there, amongst the giant stalks and their ripening fingers.

And she hurried out of the place, pulling the pram after her, taking one last look at the little curled-up creature. He looked just like a baby, turned over to the wall, all peaceful, with his hands up in the air and his palms open.

She remembered Karen and Angela; the way they slept when babies, with their hands up; open to the stars. Why were they surrendering when they had captured us?

She left the place. And she hoped that a tarantula would not come creeping out of the darkness, behind the stalks. She did not relish the thought of Parsival's testicles being eaten by a huge spider.

She was no longer floating, but coming down to earth. Her feet were heavy, were pulling her down into the melting pavement. She could hardly drag herself along.

Gloria pushed the pram back towards her precious home. You could already smell the approach of dawn. All she wanted now was to be well away from the threatening streets, before the day broke upon her.

22

She had bolted the door, and stacked the furniture against it, and now she was safe here inside her head of bricks. She and her house were one and nobody could enter.

All she had to do now was pass the time until he came.

Gloria switched on the television for the first time in months, and watched the horizontal lines making love to the verticals; it was her favourite programme.

It was morning, or so they were saying in the street. They were saying it with their assembled dead faces. 'SOMEDAY HE'LL COME ALONG, THE MAN I LOVE. AND HE'LL BE BIG AND STRONG, THE MAN I LOVE.' She looked down over the crowd, and blew them a series of kisses and understood how Her Majesty must feel, on occasions.

They were pointing. The dead had cracked their way up through the paving stones, and the buds of their faces were smiling and hooting at her. But she had nothing against them.

She was more angry with the treacherous cold that she had brought upon herself. And she knew that there was one solution. 'Wine.' She had some.

She lay down upon her divan and watched the sliver of moon whilst Signor Gigli almost burst his cheeks with song. 'Torno Sorrento—or I must die.'

Dear Benjamino, we nearly met once, in Napoli. We missed by a corner; by a corner's crooked heart. 'Farewell, sweet singer, had we met, both our lives would have been changed, radically.' She drank some wine and lifted up the telephone. 'Hello, may I speak to Phoebe Wainright?'

'Certainly. This is her skeleton speaking. Shall I get her?'

'Yes please. Incidentally, who is Phoebe Wainright?'

'A name that came out of your head.'

'May I speak to her anyway?'

'Hold on a minute. I'll get her for you.'

'Thank you very much. Goodbye.'

'Not at all. Thank you for calling. Goodbye.'

He had a very lovely voice, Benjamino Gigli.

She slammed down the dead receiver of stolen property, and wondered how she had managed to dredge up Phoebe Wainright out of her mind. Phoebe Wainright, that frail nobody who had died before she even existed.

Gloria knew that soon she would fall asleep, and she felt absolutely beautiful. She knew that she had to squirt some Mitsouku upon her flesh. The spray was near, so she did. And she was feeling so tired now. But before she could fall asleep, Moss would have to come, there was no denying the need to rendezvous with the only person she had ever loved.

She had piled the records and they were playing, one after the other, and she was thankful that there was no need to change them.

'FALLING IN LOVE WITH LOVE IS FALLING FOR MAKE BELIEVE, FALLING IN LOVE WITH LOVE IS PLAYING THE FOOL...' She simply had to have one last dance around the room before sleeping.

'What's a nice girl like you doing in a place like this?'
'I must be out of my mind, that's why.'
'You dance divinely. What's your name?'
'I mustn't talk to strangers.'
'Don't talk then; just dance.'

But the other one broke the silence first. 'May I see you home?'

She did not reply, but lifted the bottle of wine before her. The world looked much better through green glass. She banished her dancing partner before she spoke.

'Yes. I admit that it was never my real name. But my skin has become transparent tonight, and so I can reveal all. I have nothing to hide, and nowhere to hide, and someone is coming for me and I'm glad,' she raised the bottle to salute the beautiful woman in the mirror.

'To all your lovers, dead or alive, young or old. To all my lovers upon the sea or beneath it. On the earth or within it. To all your faces that I forget; those handsome faces of all the boys who loved you; rolled and merged into one. To you, Gloria, and to all the pleasure I gave you. Cheers!'

She danced out of her living-room and glided along the corridor. Into the other rooms, and out of the other rooms; down the stairs, and up the stairs. She danced and she danced. 'Men are all the same, all except Moss.'

She sat upon the lavatory, but not to do anything. Ghosts hardly ever infested lavatories. They either had a keen sense of smell, or they had a keen sense of decency.

Gloria never felt anxious upon the lavatory, for it was here she always read the colour supplements of the Sunday newspapers. For in those advertisements you could live forever and do what you like. And you were young and gay and rich and extremely beautiful. And you were wanted by those you wanted.

For a moment a real sadness descended. 'Why wasn't I born two hundred years to come, when they have already discovered the secret of immortality? And I am young and beautiful and a dancer; and my name is Jane and life is beautiful and forever. I feel I've been cheated!'

But the image of how she would never be left her, to make room for someone else. She closed her eyes and saw only Moss descending, Moss coming towards her bringing only peace.

But remembering that Moss would need to recognize her, she flew to the dressing-table, and when she placed the golden wig upon her head, she breathed more deeply.

She simply had to be all prepared for him, and as she applied the cosmetics to her face, she tried to conjure up her dead husband. But that man was most reluctant to enter the atmosphere.

'Halitosis. Poor dear, you can hardly blame him.' And his own death had not come as a terrible shock to him; he just said, in his Marlborough voice, 'I'd simply love a cup of tea, but I think I'm going to die, so it seems out of the question.' And he very gently put down his ready reckoner and snuffed it. Sean was very experienced at dying. All his life he had been dying. He had died exactly the same way on their wedding day. And more so on their wedding night. She had died also on that night. Just a little, before she came alive again. He and his kind had been her fatal flaw, until Moss.

She shifted the wig, ever so slightly, until it fitted perfectly. What she always needed was a man.

'You had an appetite for boys, Gloria, and they were

no good for you. Little baby boys. And when they grew up you sent them away, you made them leave home.' Those pretty boys had never been tempered by the fires of disappointment, failure and struggle.

It was amazing how she could control herself, despite the empty bottle. They had all fallen for her, but they were too young and too many, until Moss. And Moss was all of them, altogether.

She looked across, and she saw the shape in the hotel window opposite. He moved. It could have been Moss, but on the other hand, why would he be watching her? Why had he not come straight through the crowd outside? And why was he now hiding, flattened against a wall in the room opposite, desperately trying not to be seen by her? No, it definitely wasn't Moss.

Edith Piaf walked into the room, in no uncertain terms, and as her voice filled the house, tears filled Gloria's eyes.

'JE NE REGRETTE RIEN.'

Down in the street, the boil of the crowd was swelling, but the fishmonger beyond was entirely absorbed in his filletings.

'You'll never get me. You'll have to carry me out. I've defied you, I've beaten you. I've beaten you at last.' She did not open the window as she shouted down at the monster. It was a huge dark octopus animal below, with great hungry jaws wide open. Therefore she gave it the full weight of her fury, and as she cursed it she smiled.

Gloria went again to her reflection, for now she knew she would be absolutely safe if she just watched herself and the entire room in the mirror.

She could now see that her past might not have been so passionate. Almost all her beloved characters from that past might have been totally non-existent. She didn't mind facing all this now, and she fully admitted that there were probably great areas of her past that had been mere fantasy. But there was still time, she could yet live. She could yet build herself a beautiful future, a beautiful fabulous, passionate future, filled with the fresh air of reality. And here and there she would come across some sincere and worthy individuals, now going through this same no-man's-island. There were all kinds of lost; at least she knew she had been. But she had found herself at last.

'I can stare you out,' she said to her face. 'I'm not afraid of you, I can stare you out.' She had never really seen that face before.

'WHEN YOU WALK THROUGH A STORM KEEP YOUR HEAD UP HIGH, AND DON'T BE AFRAID OF THE DARK,' she sang to the face.

It was necessary to stare into yourself, to see beyond yourself. And it was necessary to go into yourself to get beyond yourself. There was no way around it, and there was no escaping it, so she did just that, and the face started to fall away.

The flesh came away in waves, and an army of worms came scuttling out of the bloody rotting interior. And the stark eyes stared back right into her. It was necessary to look into, and enter into, the eye of the most impossible storm. 'I've never really seen you before. I do not know you. I do not know me. How do you do?'

'How do you do,' the face answered back. It had become more coherent and nicer to look at. You had to go beyond the horrors of self, in order to see the beauty within.

'How did you get in?'

'You know how.' The voice was lower than hers, but

189

it seemed to come from within her. The strange voice belonged to her; she felt very attached to it and was not afraid.

'Don't be afraid of me.'

'You seem to know exactly what I am thinking,' she replied.

Gloria was glad they were alone, and that he had come out of the mirror to keep her company. To be alone with someone was to destroy loneliness. 'How did you get in?'

'But you knew I would, nothing could keep me out.' The voice seemed to be getting lower and lower in tone, and now he took off the wig.

Mr Moss stood before her. 'You know what I want.'

'Yes, I know what you want.'

'You know what I want, you know what I've come for.' There was great strength and deep gentleness in his voice.

'Touch me! Touch me! Nothing has ever touched me.'

His touch was so subtle, his hands were two shafts of breeze, gently clasping her shoulders and pulling her towards him.

'I'm taking you away. I've come to take you away.'

She kissed his cold smooth lips and stared deep into his eyes. His breath and hers were one.

He looked at her and held her, and he felt sorry for the sad and tired woman.

She looked at him and held him, and hoped he would love her forever. 'Say you will never leave me, never.'

He wondered why she needed to be reassured. It was obvious he would stay with her. 'I will love you forever, and never leave you,' he said.

'Shall I lie down on the bed?' she asked.

'Lie down on the bed,' he said. 'And I shall lie with you.'

'All my life I've waited for you. Tell me you love me,' she said.

'I love you! I love you, Gloria!'

'Do you really? Tell me again. Tell me again and again,' she said.

He needed to tell her what she needed to know. 'I love you! I love you! I love you!'

'All my life people have told me lies. Tell me the truth. Why have you really come?'

'I love you and I've come to take you,' he said. 'I love you. I love you forever.'

'Now! Please do it now! My life has been frigid endlessness. Make me feel something, make me feel nothing. Touch me!'

She fell backwards, slowly. And he watched from where she lay upon the bed. And he was beside her, and above her. Mr Moss had come so silently and soon he would be within her. She was waiting for him to enter her, and come inside her, so that she would burst and flow back into the universe.

'Now love me gently. Say only beautiful things to me.'

And Mr Moss descended. 'I'll do it all for you. You leave it all to me. Lie back and close your eyes, and let me enter you. And you will suffer no more.'

But she did not close her eyes, not immediately. She still wanted to see that indelible face that was so familiar. The face that was on the tip of her tongue. She could see herself in his eyes, and she could see that he would accept her for what she was.

'I love you, Gloria,' he said. 'That's right! That's right!'

'I love you, Gloria,' she said. 'I love you forever.'

'I love you, Gloria,' he said, and she said, 'Sleep now! Sleep now!'

He would stay with her tonight, and forever. And he would take her away, and she would never leave.

'It's funny, I always imagined you'd come with all the answers, but now I can't think of any questions. I love life, but I'm so tired,' she heard herself saying.

'I know you do.'

'Yes, I know you. I do.' And she or he did not know who was talking, they were so close now.

'Darling, oh darling. The smell of leaves and wood and dampness. And your lips are cold. Please take me faster and faster. Now! Now! Now! Up me, up me, up me. Right up me! Burst inside me, make me lose myself. Take me, take me, take me. Love me and destroy me. Destroy me. Yes, yes. Like this. Thank you! It's blinding daylight. All the dark is gone.'

The sky exploded, cracking the banks of time.

The sun burst within her and all was peace.